ROBERT B. PARKER'S
REVENGE TOUR

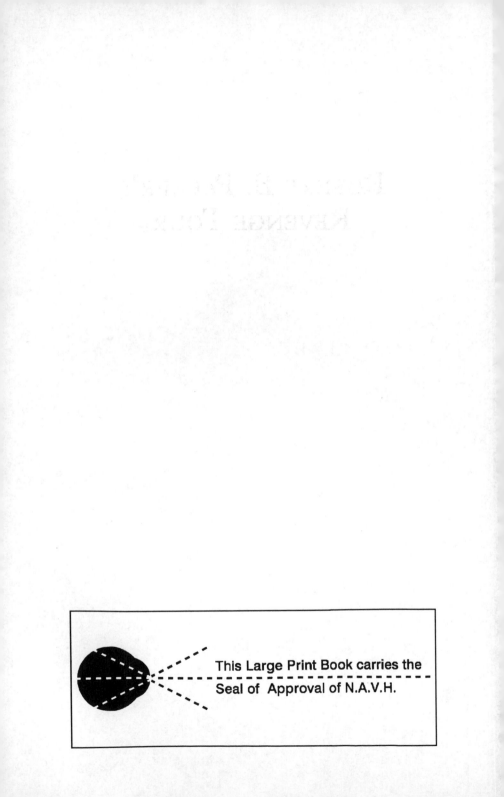

This Large Print Book carries the
Seal of Approval of N.A.V.H.

A SUNNY RANDALL NOVEL

ROBERT B. PARKER'S REVENGE TOUR

MIKE LUPICA

THORNDIKE PRESS
A part of Gale, a Cengage Company

GALE
A Cengage Company

LIBRARY OF CONGRESS CIP DATA ON FILE.
CATALOGUING IN PUBLICATION FOR THIS BOOK
IS AVAILABLE FROM THE LIBRARY OF CONGRESS.

ISBN-13: 978-1-4328-9687-4 (hardcover alk. paper)

Published in 2022 by arrangement with G. P. Putnam's Sons, an imprint of Penguin Publishing Group, a division of Penguin Random House LLC.

Printed in Mexico
Print Number: 01   Print Year: 2022

This book is for Peter Gethers.

ONE

"I don't know why they just couldn't leave well enough alone," Phil Randall said to me.

"Dad," I said, "I'm pretty sure you said the same thing when they broke up the phone company."

We were seated at a window table in The Street Bar at The Newbury, which had been the old Ritz before it became the Taj. Then one of the big hotel chains had bought the property and closed it down for a couple years and done a renovation that I was certain had cost more than Bill Gates's divorce. When I'd learned the dollar figures on both of them, I'd idly wondered how my life would have turned out if I'd married one of those men, and not a child of the Boston Mob.

We were drinking martinis just because it seemed to be the thing to do. The quality of the martinis at The Street Bar hadn't improved as much as the condition of the hotel, which really had needed one of those extreme makeovers. But the quality of the martinis hadn't diminished, either. My father had told them to use Beluga Gold, informing me as he often did that you only live once.

"Don't get me started on phones," he said. "I liked the world a lot better when the only things I needed when I left the house were a gun and badge, and not an iPhone ninety-nine."

He had been one of the best and most decorated detectives in the history of the Boston Police Department. And still thought of himself as a cop. And, bless his heart, always would.

"Think you might be slightly off on your math there," I said. "I think we're only working on the iPhone fifty at this point."

"I am making a larger point about the modern world," he said.

"As you so often do."

"Let me tell you another thing about cell phones," he said, shaking his head disgustedly. "Text messaging is the devil's handiwork."

I grinned at him, an almost permanent condition for me when in his presence. "How do you feel about apps?"

"App this," my father said.

He drank. I drank. It was the height of the cocktail hour, but I knew the bartender from when the place was still the Taj. So we had scored the best of the handful of window tables in the place. Every other table was occupied. So were the stools at the bar, on the other side of the room, to your left as you walked in from a lobby far more ornate than it had been before. No more masks. No more social distancing. Somehow it made everything in a wonderful old capital of the Back Bay feel new again, which is exactly what the owners of The Newbury had been shooting for, on a rather grand scale. I hadn't priced out the rooms, but suspected that before booking one I would have had to sell jewelry if I wanted the weekend package.

"And I frankly don't understand why they had to move the entrance to the hotel around the corner," Phil Randall said.

"If they hadn't," I said, "we'd be sitting at The Arlington."

"Cute," he said.

"You've always thought so."

"You better believe it, kid," he said.

We raised our glasses at the same moment. He smiled at me. His smile was either elfin or impish, I'd never been able to decide which best described him. Truth was, the cute one was him.

"At least the view from here remains the same," he said, staring across Arlington at the Public Garden.

"Well," I said, "until they build that cell tower they're thinking of building next to the statue of George Washington."

"Is that supposed to be funny?"

I said, "Apparently not."

He wore a tweed Brooks Brothers jacket and a button-down blue shirt with the Brooks roll to the collar and a bright red silk tie and pocket square to match the tie. He smelled of bay rum. He was getting older; it was happening more quickly than I would have wished. Just not older to me.

I noticed him looking past me now at the entrance to the bar, frowning, as if suddenly putting his cop eyes to use.

"What?" I said, swiveling my head around.

"Nothing," he said. "Just thought I saw someone I know."

"Friend or foe?" I said.

"Little bit of both," he said, then dismissed the subject with a wave of his hand. "But then my vision isn't what it used to be."

"Like hell it's not," I said.

And we drank. I was so happy to be at this table, in this room, with him. I wasn't all that keen on the male species these days.

But Phil Randall was a notable exception. As was Spike.

It was as if my father were reading my mind.

"How's Richie?" he said.

Richie Burke. Ex-husband.

"We had dinner the other night," I said. "He wants to start dating again."

"Good!" my father said.

"I told him no."

"Why would you do something as short-sighted as that?"

"Because I don't want for us to get back together," I said. "At least not in that way. And it's time for me to meet somebody new."

"Well," he said, "a father can hope."

"Despite half a lifetime trying to put *his* father in jail," I said.

Desmond Burke. It was silly to think of him as being the head of the Irish Mob in Boston. At this point in time, he *was* the Irish Mob in Boston.

"Don't take this the wrong way," Phil Randall said, "but you aren't getting any younger."

"I'm sorry," I said. "Is there a *right* way for a girl to take that?"

I rose out of my chair just enough and leaned across the table to kiss him on top of his head. *Yup,* I thought. *Definitely bay rum.*

"I just think you need a man in your life," he said.

"Okay," I said, "that's it, you're under arrest, in the name of modern women everywhere."

He laughed. I laughed. As always, he made me feel that everything was going to be all right, whatever happened to be going on in my life.

"I just remembered," he said, "you told me you had something you wanted to tell me about a new client."

"As a matter of fact, I do," I said. "A new old one. Like the hotel."

"And who might that be?"

"Melanie Joan Hall," I said.

"Your landlord?"

"I think she prefers best-selling, world-famous author," I said.

"Isn't she the one who nearly got my baby girl killed that time?"

"One and the same."

"So what's the good news?" my father said.

TWO

Before we left the bar I tried to correct the record with my father about what had actually transpired when I had first been hired by Melanie Joan Hall.

She was being stalked by an especially creepy ex-husband with even creepier sexual tastes. But Richie and I had teamed up to finally take him down, and an equally dangerous friend along with him, when they tried to drug and assault me, not knowing I had shown up having taken an antidote.

"Good times," Phil Randall said drily.

But Melanie Joan had shown her undying gratitude to Rosie the dog and me by allowing us to rent her four-story town house on River Street Place, where, legend had it, ship sails had been woven in the long-ago. Melanie Joan had once again fallen in love at that particular moment in her life and had gone Hollywood, something that seemed as inevitable to me as the phases of

13

the moon. She wanted me to live in the town house rent-free. I told her I couldn't do that. She finally established a ridiculously low figure as an alternative and wouldn't take no for an answer. Saying no to Melanie Joan, queen of the bodice-ripping romance novels and founder of what called itself, without the slightest hint of irony, the Ardor Channel, was like trying to stop the rain.

So she had gone off years ago to, in her words, put even more tinsel in Tinseltown, and Rosie and I had lived at the foot of Beacon Hill ever since.

"Tell me she doesn't want her house back," my father said, "even though your mother has kept your room as you left it."

"Just neater, I'm guessing."

"There's that."

"You're too old to move back home," he said.

"And, in your view, not getting any younger."

He waved for the check. I told him this one was on me. While we waited I explained to him that the Ardor Channel, the mention of which always made him giggle, was about to start shooting a new series based on Melanie Joan's most recent book, the first one set in the modern world, one chronicling the adventures of the great-

14

granddaughter of her signature character, Cassandra Demeter, the spunky and extremely frisky girl from the wrong side of the tracks in Boston who had made it into the thick of Brahmin society at the turn of the century. With and without her clothes on.

"Your mother loves those books," my father said. "God save us and protect us."

"Melanie Joan is actually staying here at the hotel," I said. "I'm meeting her for dinner at Davio's."

"You two walking over together?"

"What, and spoil her entrance?"

"She should have joined us for a drink," he said.

"Would have cut into essential prep time for hair and makeup and wardrobe," I said.

"Why does she need you this time?"

"Says she has a problem only I can help her with."

"Hopefully not one that puts you in harm's way."

I sighed. "I can take care of myself."

"If I had a nickel," Phil Randall said.

When I'd signed the check, I saw him once again staring over at the entrance to The Street Bar again.

"You okay?"

"Never better," he said.

He had parked in a lot at Exeter and Newbury, saying the walk would do him good, he could get some air and walk off the vodka before he got into the car. I told him I was going to take a stroll through the Public Garden before making my way back to Davio's.

I kissed him on the cheek when we were outside and standing in front of the new entrance to the hotel.

"You're sure you're okay?" I said.

"I just told you I was," he said. "And you know I never lie to my baby girl."

While I waited for the light to change on Arlington, I turned around, already smiling, expecting to see my father's jaunty walk as he made his way down my favorite walking street in the whole city.

But he was already gone.

Wherever he was going, it wasn't to his car.

And as for him never lying to his baby girl, it would turn out that there was a first time for everything.

THREE

Of course Melanie Joan had arranged for us to be seated at a table that seemed to be the exact geographic center of the front room, in the most visible and best-lit part of Davio's. Of course she showed up a half-hour late.

While I waited alone at the table, I pondered the fact that this was what passed for a big night out for me these days, first with my father and now with the author of her current best seller, *Burning Excess.*

When Melanie Joan did finally show up, I saw that she had on a bright red dress and a hat I could have sworn had been worn by the woman whose horse had recently won the Kentucky Derby, and won Spike a whole pile of money in the process.

It was like every entrance I'd ever seen her make, into any room, including the ladies' room. I wasn't sure how many people in the room knew exactly who she was. Just that she was Somebody. At least some of the women turning their heads to follow her slow progress toward our table on the arm of the manager, Armando, surely had to recognize their favorite author, whether they admitted that or not. It was unlikely that any of the men did. Martha Stewart probably had more male readers than Melanie Joan Hall did.

"Please sit down!" Melanie Joan commanded when I stood to greet her, rising up out of what must have looked to the room like a supplicant's chair. "I don't want everybody to think I'm having dinner with my *daughter.*"

She quickly air-kissed me in the general vicinity of both cheeks. I couldn't identify her scent as easily as I had my father's, just knew instantly that it was pretty damned wonderful.

We had been given a table for four. Melanie Joan took off her hat and placed it on the chair next to her. Somehow not a single hair was out of place after she did.

"You look beautiful, Melanie Joan," I said to her.

She smiled, almost sadly, I thought.

"What was it that Scott Fitzgerald said at the end of *Gatsby*?" she said. "We beat on, boats against the current, borne back ceaselessly to our plastic surgeon."

"Pretty sure it's borne back into the past," I said.

"Oh, don't I wish, darling."

It had been more than two years since I'd last seen her, when she'd stopped in Boston on her last book tour. I assumed she'd had more work done since then, but, as always, it had been artfully done. Being a trained detective, I knew how old she was, and at the same time knew how difficult she'd made it to find out her actual age online.

But to be in the age range she very much wanted people to think she was, only sneaking up on AARP, her first novel would have to have been published when she was in the third grade.

It was clear, once the small talk began, that she would be taking her time telling me why we were here, despite having made it sound like a matter of life and death.

"How's your cute better half?" she said.

I grinned. "Rosie?"

"You know who I mean."

Apparently everybody except our waiter wanted to talk about Richie Burke tonight. Somehow he was with me even when he wasn't, as if we were together even when we were not.

"Richie's fine. And no, we're not."

"Not what?"

"Not doing what you were about to ask if we're doing."

"And what about your *other* other?"

"If you are referring to Chief Stone," I said, "he is currently doing what I'm not doing with Richie with a red-haired vixen named Rita Fiore."

"The lawyer?" Melanie Joan said. "I believe I used her one time."

"Well, now Jesse is."

"Now, now," she said. "All's fair in sex and war."

She ordered a cosmopolitan and insisted that I join her. From past experience, I knew it was best to acquiesce. And I'd always thought cosmos were yummy. I knew she would get to what she needed to get to at her own pace. *Hey,* I thought. *She's the writer.*

Melanie Joan raised her glass when the drinks arrived and proposed a toast to strong, single women.

"Yes, to us," I said, feeling as if I ought to chime in.

"I was only talking about you," she said.

She put down her long-stemmed glass then. And in that moment, she was no longer the glam queen of Fem Lit and burning loins, as the sculpted and perfectly

20

made-up face turned almost solemn.

"So," she said.

She was staring past me, as if something completely fascinating were happening at the raw bar.

I waited.

"I really am afraid I'm in trouble again, Sunny," she said.

"Tell me about it," I said.

"I'd rather not," she said.

"Force yourself," I said.

"We can talk about it after dinner."

"I can manage both," I said. "I'm the kind of multitasker that makes young multitaskers aspirational."

"It's not funny!" she said in a voice loud enough that I saw people at the nearest tables do some head-swiveling.

"I'll be better able to judge that when I know what 'it' is," I said.

She lowered her voice now, leaned forward. Fewer lines in her forehead than when I'd last saw her. I hadn't given in to Botox. Yet.

"Someone has accused me of literary theft," she said.

I let that settle for just a moment before I said, "Who?"

"I don't know."

"What do they want?"

"I don't know that, either."
Piece of cake, I thought.

FOUR

We were back at The Newbury in her penthouse suite, having walked back from Davio's, where I was afraid Armando might be considering a career change or perhaps even witness protection after seeing how little of our black cod each of us had eaten.

Now Melanie Joan was on her couch, feet up, sipping a brandy, telling me again how awful it all was.

"I feel as if that was well established before we left the restaurant," I said.

"Don't be snarky."

I smiled. "Make me."

At least she smiled back.

"I did not steal the idea for Cassandra!" she said, and not for the first time.

Cassandra Demeter, of course. The character Melanie Joan talked about as if she were quite real, and had made her quite famous. And stupidly rich.

"I believe you," I said, also not for the first

time, not that it seemed to provide any consolation.

Even with all of her theatrical starts and stops, I now knew Melanie Joan's problem. Someone had contacted her via email, telling her that the novel that had put Melanie Joan on the literary map had originally been written by someone else.

"This awful person told me that Cassandra is somebody else's work and he can prove it," she said. "And that there would be no new character for the new TV show if I hadn't stolen the idea for Cassandra in the first place."

"The great-granddaughter," I said. "That new character."

"Destiny," she said.

It was the name of the great-granddaughter, not an assessment of her current circumstances.

A sigh came out of Melanie Joan now that sounded more mournful than a country song. She might have started crying if she wasn't worried about what it might do to her makeup.

"Has anybody ever accused you of plagiarism before?" I said.

"Don't use that awful word!"

She took a big slug of brandy.

"Okay, let's back up," I said. "Whose

24

content is it that you are supposed to have taken?"

"He won't say," I said. "Just that he has proof."

"You know it's a man who's been contacting you?"

"I just assumed," she said. "They've caused most of the problems in my life, haven't they?"

Now I sighed.

"Don't you use that tone with me," she said.

The bottle of brandy was on the coffee table between us. I imagined myself grabbing it and drinking from it straight.

"Are you aware of something called Guerilla Mail?" Melanie Joan said.

Actually I was. It was an encrypted mail provider that had come up in a case I'd worked the previous year in Los Angeles involving a noted agent, and former boyfriend of sorts, named Tony Gault.

"And you got this email last week?" I said.
She nodded.

"May I see it?"

"I trashed it," she said.

"Untrash it, please," I said.

"I'm quite sure I deleted it *after* I trashed it."

"I'll go into your mail later and un-delete

it," I said. "For now, why don't you just try to remember it as close to word for word as you can."

Now she reached for the bottle of brandy. She had offered me some before. But I knew enough about myself to know that if I started drinking brandy with her, this might turn into a sleepover.

"This person said that they knew what I had done and that *I* knew what I had done," Melanie Joan said. "And the pain I'd caused *because* of what I'd done, and not just to the original author."

"And whoever this is," I said, "they're looking for money?"

She put her head back and closed her eyes and now looked every minute of the age I knew she was.

"I'm just assuming," she said, "even if the turgid prose concluded with me being told that in the end, it was going to cost me *more* than money."

She got up and walked to the window, glass in hand, and stared at the lights beyond the park.

"I simply cannot have this at this stage of my life," she said. "Or, for that matter, *any* stage of my life. For a writer, even the suggestion that you might have done something like this really is a fate worse than death."

"But you didn't do it," I said.

She wheeled to face me.

"It won't matter!" she snapped. "It will be as if I'm wearing a scarlet letter."

Then she told me the story of a noted romance novelist who had once been caught ripping off an even more famous and successful romance novelist. I was vaguely aware of both names.

"What happened?" I said.

"The woman who got caught had to write a big check is what happened," Melanie Joan said. "She announced that a psychological disorder had made her do it, and got by with that well enough to resume her career, even though sales were never the same after that." Melanie Joan seemed to sag. "And then she died."

She sat back down on the couch.

"Please promise me that you'll make this go away," she said. "You must understand that for a writer, this is like being MeToo'ed."

There were more questions that I knew needed to be asked. A lot more. I knew there was much she was not telling me. But I could see her starting to shut down. So I told her we would revisit this in the morning. She made me promise again that I would make it go away, the way I had once

27

made her ex-husband go away, and for a long time. I told her I would try. She said that I had to do better than that.

I took the elevator down and walked around the park and up to Beacon before making a left on Charles, and then past the Charles Street Meeting House toward home. I stopped at one point and turned around, thinking that someone might be following me. But saw no one.

Probably just my imagination.

What happened when you hung around with a writer.

Occupational hazard, for both of us.

FIVE

Melanie Joan's current agent, Samantha Heller, was in my office over P. F. Chang's at ten the next morning, for the meeting she had requested and one to which I had readily agreed. It had been only one night with Melanie Joan, but I was already looking for as much backup as I could find.

Samantha was very pretty and if she was somewhere in my demographic, she was carrying it off very well. If I knew that Melanie Joan went through agents the way she did husbands, Ms. Heller had to be aware of that fact as well. But she seemed to be one sharp cookie.

Could even women call other women cookies anymore?

Maybe Samantha would know.

She was blond, and taller than me. I'd always wanted to be taller than me. She was wearing a short leather jacket and jeans and also had a better figure than I did. We hadn't even started working together yet and I was wondering if I needed to hate her.

"Having known some of Melanie Joan's previous representatives," I said, "you're not exactly what I expected."

She only made things worse for herself, at least from where I was sitting, by smiling a winner of a cover-girl smile.

"I'm told I sound much older on the phone," she said.

"Your predecessors were, ah, slightly more mature, as I recall," I said.

She held the smile. "Spoiler alert," she said. "They ended up being just more ugly divorces for MJ."

"Kind of her thing."

Samantha Heller said, "She thought I might be better suited to tap into the zeitgeist."

"I've always wondered," I said, "if that was something you could actually do."

She laughed. Her Prada bag had been dropped casually next to one of my client chairs. Her Golden Goose sneakers had the proper worn-in look, as if they'd first been worn by her mother. Whether we could actually work comfortably together was yet to be determined. But I could see already we could shop together.

Forget about hating her. I was starting to

think it might be love. I asked how she became an agent. She laughed again and said, "Practice, practice, practice," then told me she had bounced around a bit after college, before taking an entry-level job at McArdle and Lowell, Melanie Joan's publisher. She'd finally become an assistant to Melanie Joan's editor, then when Melanie Joan had fired yet another agent, it seemed like a natural fit for her to make the switch.

"Forget about me," she said. "MJ made you sound like some sort of superhero."

"No," I said, "but my best friend is. His name is Spike."

"I think Melanie Joan mentioned him," she said. "He's gay, right?"

"He tries not to make a big thing out of it."

"She says he has everything except a cape."

"He brings the cape out for Halloween, unless I beg him not to."

I asked her how she came to this moment. "At the agency or in life?" she said.

"Life," I said.

"I am a child of the Upper East Side of New York City," she said. She smiled again. "I'm almost proud to say."

"Oh," I said. "*That* old place."

"Dalton," she said. "NYU, because I

31

didn't make the cut at Columbia, but couldn't bring myself to leave the big, bad city. Only moved to Boston because I had a shot at McArdle and Lowell. Finally did the agent thing at Quill. Our agency. Graduated from there to a master's degree in Melanie Joan Hall."

"What's your ultimate goal?" I said.

"Other than world domination?" she said.

I offered her coffee. She said tea if I had some. I told her that she was in luck, I had tea pods for my Keurig. I made a cup for her and Dunkin' decaf coffee for myself. I'd already had so much caffeine in me this morning I'd considered challenging my Peloton trainer to a fistfight.

I heard her phone chirp from inside the bag. She didn't grab for it as if it might go off. Before long we'd be picking out furniture.

"How much did she tell you?" Samantha asked.

"Enough to know how frightened she is," I said. "About somebody coming after her this way, even more about it getting out."

"Even though she says it's a lie," Samantha said. "We both know it *is* a lie, right?"

"I think 'know' might be a bit strong," I said. I put air quotes around *know*. "But I'm ever hopeful."

Samantha smiled again. "For better or worse," she said, "Melanie Joan swears she has always written her own breathless prose."

"I thought it was deathless prose."

"Have it your way," she said.

She had blue eyes the color of sapphires. As hurtful as the notion was, I saw her as a younger version of me. Blonder. And taller. God damn it.

"What I'm trying to wrap my head around," I said, "is that if she is being blackmailed, why no demand?"

"This has only been going on for a week or so," Samantha said. "For now, MJ feels as if this person is more interested in scaring the living shit out of her. And succeeding, I might add."

"Yeah," I said. "Based off of my time with her last night, mission accomplished."

"It really is as if she's being stalked all over again," she said, "before you rescued the fair maiden that time."

"She told you about that?"

"She tells everybody," Samantha said.

The phone chirped again. This time she reached in, looked at the screen, nodded, casually tossed it back into the bag. Obviously even her steely will had limits. Sometimes I could go as long as two or three minutes without checking from whom a missed call had come.

"Not important?" I said.

"Depends on who you ask," she said. "The great and powerful Richard Gross is trying to reach me. MJ's lawyer. And manager. You've heard of him."

"I spent a lot of time on a case in Los Angeles last year," I said. "They call him Gross Points out there, if I'm not mistaken."

"I'm impressed."

"I've been known to check out *The Hollywood Reporter,*" I said.

"Look at you," she said.

"Richard Gross has only been repping Melanie Joan for a few years, right?" I said.

"For a while I was afraid she might marry him," she said.

"What's he like?" I said. "Gross."

She laughed. *"Gross,"* she said.

"You two don't get along?'

Samantha said, "Richard doesn't think she needs an agent, having now been blessed to have him in her world."

"I'll bet he can tap into the zeitgeist," I said.

"Only if he thinks there really are points for him on the back end," she said.

The phone chirped again. She ignored it again, and drank more of her tea. "So what do you think you can do?" Samantha asked. "Before things escalate."

"Sounds as if that happened as soon as she got the email," I said. "And just so we're clear. You *are* convinced there is no possible way that she stole material, even when she was just getting started."

She ran a hand through her hair. Mine had been that color once, in a shade I thought of as the original Sunny.

"Is it possible that there is someone out there who conceived a character they think strongly resembles Cassandra Demeter?" she said. "Sure. Even when we send one of Melanie Joan's books out in Hollywood, and even though it's someone as well known as her, we sometimes hear there are three other people pitching something similar."

"But if it is true," I said, "the injured person waited a long time to get even, right?"

"And must think they have a good reason to somehow get even with her," she said. "A *very* good reason."

Now it was my phone, the landline on my desk, ringing. The noise was loud enough to startle us both.

"Sunny Randall," I said when I answered.

"He's been in my room!" Melanie Joan shouted from her end of the call, right

35

before Samantha Heller and I were on our
way to The Newbury.

Six

She was waiting for us when we got out of the elevator at the penthouse level, twitchy as a hummingbird, dressed in workout clothes I knew weren't cheap, just because nothing Melanie Joan Hall owned ever was.

The baseball cap she was wearing had ARDOR written on the front.

"It took the two of you long enough!" she snapped.

"Melanie Joan," Samantha said, her voice calm. "We were at Sunny's office. It's on the other side of the park. We felt it was quicker to walk. Or run, to be more precise."

"We're here now," I said.

"Well," Melanie Joan said, "hooray for both of you."

We walked down to her suite, at the end of a long hallway. She used her key card to let us all in. I knew it was challenging in the world of key cards to break into a hotel room. But my friend Ghost Garrity, who had elevated breaking and entering into an art form, had explained to me one time that if you could get your hands on a used card to start the process, it wasn't as difficult as you might think.

"Look!" Melanie Joan said, pointing dramatically at the coffee table where her bottle of Emperador, specially ordered for her by The Newbury, had rested the night before.

In the middle of the table was a copy of *Burning Excess,* her latest book, red paint that was apparently supposed to look like blood splashed across the cover, a sharp-point paring knife driven into the book.

Samantha Heller started to reach down and I told her not to touch anything, just in case prints had been left, though I doubted that they had.

Melanie Joan told us that she'd just come back from her morning walk when she found the book and the knife.

"It wasn't there before you left?" I said.

"Of course it wasn't!"

"Have you called hotel security?" I said to Melanie Joan.

"I called you!" she said. "Do you think I want to read about this on Page Six?"

We were in Boston and Page Six was the gossip section of the *New York Post.* But we

38

both knew what she was saying.

"We should get them up here," I said.

"Absolutely not!" she said. "Once something like this gets out, people will immediately want to know why someone would do something as hideous as this."

I knew that I would have to talk to the hotel, and sooner rather than later, because they'd want to look at footage from the video cameras I knew had to be situated in the hall. But I also knew that if you were tech-savvy enough to manufacture a key card at a high-end hotel, then you could get yourself a jammer for the cameras. I'd seen it done before, and not just at places like The Newbury.

For now, I was making the assumption that if somebody had risked making a delivery like this, that person was no amateur. Or, in the words of my sainted father, had brass ones.

"We may need bodyguards for the rest of your stay in Boston," Samantha Heller said.

"Sunny has guarded me before," Melanie Joan said. "She can do it again."

No no no, I thought.

Fuck no.

But then Samantha Heller, bless her heart, threw me a life preserver.

"We're going to be fighting a two-front

battle here, Melanie Joan," she said to her client. "I'm not sure Sunny can handle this all herself."

I wondered if Melanie Joan even heard the tone Samantha was using, someone so much younger than she was speaking to her the way she would a child.

"Job one is keeping you safe," Samantha continued. "Then Sunny has to find out who is behind this nastiness. And as formidable a presence as I can already see that Sunny is, she really can't do both."

In that moment, she sounded like *my* agent.

"Sunny did both before," Melanie Joan said.

"Back then," I said, "we both knew who was after you. We didn't need to establish a list of suspects. We had our guy from the start."

Dr. John Melvin. Psychiatrist. Ex-husband. Stalker and kink. Recently turned down yet again, as emphatically as ever, by the state's parole board. It had become a very nice habit with them.

"Have you heard from your ex lately?" I said.

"No," Melanie Joan said. "And may my ex never be an ex-*con*."

"Have you?"

"Have I what?" she said, perhaps already moving on to her next thought.

"Heard from John Melvin."

"I hadn't heard from him in years," she said. "He used to write me when he first got to prison. But out of the blue, a couple months ago, a mean letter arrived at my home in L.A."

"What did it say?"

"That one day we would meet again, in one way or another."

"That was it?"

"Oh," she said, waving her hand, "there was some silliness at the end about me continuing to enjoy my success while I still could."

Samantha Heller said, "You never mentioned that to me."

"I didn't think it was worth mentioning, with him locked away," Melanie Joan said.

Samantha Heller looked at me and did a quick, subtle eye roll.

"And now I want that book out of this room this instant!" Melanie Joan said, staring at it the way she would a cockroach.

"For now, it's evidence," I said. "I'll bag it before I leave and get it to a friend of mine with the cops."

We walked into the next room, a small dining area, and sat at the table. I had

41

Melanie Joan take me through her morning. She said she had taken her morning walk down Newbury to Mass Ave. and then back up Boylston. Then again. Proudly pointing out that she made sure to walk at least three miles a day whenever possible.

"I don't keep the weight off by wishing it away," she said.

"Few can," I said.

She gave me a look that would have been far more withering if she weren't once again asking me to save her from the bad guys.

"Snarky as ever," she said.

"Chronically," I said. "Happily. Proudly."

She kept going, saying she'd finally stopped to pick up a latte at the Starbucks on the corner of Boylston and Berkeley. She said it was the morning and the sidewalks were already crowded with people going to work, and she saw no reason to be afraid, not knowing that she would become terrified as soon as she was back in the suite and saw the book. Had called me immediately, the stakes having been raised, and exponentially, in that moment.

"Maybe it is John," Melanie Joan said. "Maybe this is some kind of act of vengeance from prison. He knows that every time he has applied for parole, I have written a letter reminding the board of what he did to me. And tried to do to Sunny."

"I could make a call to the prison," I said. "All prison calls are recorded."

"But wouldn't he have been the one who waited an awfully long time to get even?" Samantha said. "Like the author of the email to our author?"

"Revenge is a powerful, and sustainable, emotion," I said. "And motivator."

"He hates us both," Melanie Joan said. "And Richie, too."

I said, "I'm going to have to start somewhere. Might as well start there. He could easily have hired someone to send that email. Perhaps he has even figured out a way to send them himself on Guerilla Mail, and hired someone to leave the book here."

I walked out of the dining area and into Melanie Joan's bedroom, went into her closet, and came out with one of the plastic dry-cleaning bags. Went back and picked up my non-Prada leather bag where I'd left it in the living room and pulled out my nitrile crime scene gloves. Then I carefully placed the book and the knife inside the dry-cleaning bag.

I knew I would call Lee Farrell at Homicide when I got back to my office and ask for another favor involving a case that had anything to do with him, or with Homicide.

I planned to do all that when, despite Melanie Joan's objections, I had gotten in touch with whomever was in charge of security at The Newbury and explained what had happened, and asked to see the video footage from her floor, beginning from when she'd gone out for her walk.

I had forgotten to take off the gloves when I came back to the dining room table.

"You carry those gloves around with you?" Samantha Heller said.

"Doesn't everybody?" I said.

"Listen," she said, "before you leave, maybe you could point me in the direction of the best private security firm in Boston."

I told her I had a better idea.

SEVEN

A couple hours later I was with Spike at what I insisted on calling the new and improved Spike's, his increasingly trendy place on Marshall Street.

"Would you call the Union Oyster House new and improved if it had been stolen by a skeevy hedge-fund asshat and then fire-bombed after that for good measure?" he asked.

"Would that the Union Oyster House never has to find out," I said.

"Let's *not* drink to that," Spike said.

We both had Virgin Marys in front of us. Spike's had been opened for about an hour. The lunch crowd was as loud and brisk as ever. The truth was that business at Spike's was better than ever, having survived the hedge-fund guy, some even worse Russians, and the fire-bombing that had ensued.

"Stop me if you've heard this one," I said.

"But I've got a situation and could use your help."

"You got it, girlfriend," he said.

"You didn't ask what the situation was."

"Don't have to," Spike said. "Don't care."

He had buzzed his hair again, shaved his beard, gained back the weight he'd lost when he thought Spike's had closed forever. He had just returned from Canyon Ranch in the Berkshires with his current boyfriend, the host of Boston's hottest morning TV show. I'd told him he was positively glowing. He told me to shut it, and just think of him as the new and improved Spike.

I filled him in now on what was happening with Melanie Joan, and the threatening email, and book, and knife. I had already dropped the book and knife with Lee Farrell at police headquarters. The red stuff was paint, which Lee said was Sherwin-Williams Rosedust, he was almost positive.

"How can you know that?" I said on the phone.

"I'm gay," he said.

"Forgot," I said.

"Ha!" he said.

Before I had driven over to Schroeder Plaza to see Lee, I had spoken with the ex-cop whom The Newbury had hired before their grand reopening to run security. Jerry

46

Flint was his name.

"Our man Flint," I'd said.

"Gee," he'd said. "I never heard that one before."

Flint told me that I was wasting my time; he already knew that there had been a ten-minute period, one that began with the time Melanie Joan said she'd left the suite, when their entire video system had gone down before rebooting.

Spike leaned forward, after carefully moving our glasses to the side.

"May I ask what may sound like a cynical question?" he said.

"It would be so unlike you."

"Might Melanie Joan, a noted drama queen, be doing this to generate attention for herself?" he said. "And buzz for her new series in the process?"

"The thought has occurred," I said.

"How can it not, for fuck's sake?" he said.

He ate some of his celery stalk. Then an olive. Even without vodka, his Marys were fully loaded, and came in hot.

"But I honestly don't think so," I said. "She's always going to be like one of her own unreliable narrators. But she's made no attempt to hide how truly geeked she is by all of this, especially after finding what she found when she got back to the room."

"It really is like she's become like a character in one of her books," Spike said.

"Or the person coming after her is," I said. "Playing the part of the villain."

"So what's the favor?" Spike said. "Even though it's silly for us to even use a term like that. I just look at it as me continuing to pay off a debt to you I will be paying off for the rest of my *fabulous* life."

He gayed up the way he said "fabulous," stretching the word halfway across the front room.

"Now you shut it," I said. "After all the times you helped me, or saved my ass, we're even. And will be even from now until the end of time."

"Still waiting to hear what it is you want me to do."

"I'd like you to keep an eye on her for a few days," I said. "As big an ask as that is."

"Not when I'm going this good."

"Only during the day," I said.

"Done," he said. "But who watches her at night?"

"I'd normally think she's safe once she calls it a night at the hotel," I said. "But the best thing would be for her to move in with me, which means moving back into her own house for the rest of her stay in Boston."

"And how long is that?"

"Couple weeks, tops," I said.

"You're willing to do that?"

"She's been awfully generous to Rosie and me," I said. "I feel as if I'd be paying off *my* debt to her."

"Not like she doesn't already owe you."

"What can I say," I said. "I'm a giver."

"Richie doesn't think so."

"It's amazing to me how, in the course of my day, and even with people I love, Richie finds his way into the conversation," I said to Spike.

"Gee," he said. "Why do you think?"

"Do you know something I don't?"

"Often," Spike said.

"Back to Melanie Joan," I said. "We good?"

He ate my last olive.

"As we like to sing at Fenway," he said, "so good, so good, so good. I've missed sleuthing with my friend Sunny."

I told him that when he put it that way, I was practically doing him the favor.

He asked me what my next stop was.

"Prison," I said.

"It was inevitable," Spike said.

EIGHT

I wasn't entirely surprised that John Melvin, formerly John Melvin, M.D., before he was stripped of his license, had agreed to see me.

He had always been a smug and arrogant bastard, one who had violated or ignored every canon of psychotherapy on his way to becoming a sexual predator and murderer, one obsessed with Melanie Joan. And with me before he was finally locked up. He'd also thought of himself as being more charming than a gigolo. Maybe it was a skill that served him well with the other inmates.

Were there even gigolos any longer? Maybe my father was right about me getting old.

He was still housed at the Massachusetts Correction Institution in Concord, known as MCI-Concord. Before I'd left Spike's the day before, Spike had asked me if I really believed Melvin could be puppet-mastering

50

another stalking of Melanie Joan, this time as a guest of the state. I told him that I wasn't sure, but that he had once been obsessed with Melanie Joan and perhaps still was, *had* stalked her himself once, and seemed to have hated her the longest. Maybe old habits really did die hard.

When I'd first put eyes on him, at a book signing in Shaker Heights, Ohio, there was nothing memorable about him. He seemed harmless enough. Of course, he was anything but. The next time I had laid eyes on him he had used his own blood as an instrument of terror against Melanie Joan, sliding his bloody hands down a window outside another bookstore, this one, as I recalled, in Cincinnati.

There were still a lot of visitor protocols that had been put in place in prisons since COVID. So it took a fair amount of time and form-filling-out for me to end up in the visitors' room for what was known as a contact visit. He was on one side of the table. I was on the other.

Since I had last seen him the day of his sentencing, he had aged, I was pleased to see, terribly. Long gone were the black-framed glasses he'd worn that first night in Ohio, and the square face. No longer Clark Kent. Maybe Father Time now, hair worn long and totally white. Wild, scraggly white beard. His face was a paler shade of gray than the gray jumpsuit he was wearing. As a child of television, I was hoping for orange. All in all, based purely on appearances, prison had not been kind to John Melvin. But in my experience, prison rarely was kind to anyone.

Somehow, though, once we started talking he acted as if he were still the knowing and confident therapist that he once had been, especially with the women he treated, before he tried to rape them. He still gave me the creeps.

"Ms. Randall," he said in his deep voice. "What an unexpected pleasure for you to have reached out to me this way. You've aged well."

"Wish I could say the same for you," I said.

"And so we begin," he said.

He smiled.

"I'm a changed man," he said. "And one of these days, when the members of the parole board finally come to their senses, I fully expect to get the opportunity to prove that to society. Maybe even to my ex-wife. And you, of course. I finally have a good lawyer. Would you like to hear about him?"

"Not even a little bit."

I waited. Waiting was always good. Especially with someone who loved the sound of his voice the way John Melvin did. Melanie Joan had once told me that he wouldn't shut up in bed, either. I assumed it was true, even if that was way too much information.

"So to what *do* I owe this pleasure?" Melvin said.

"I was just curious, being a constantly curious person," I said, "if after all this time you have decided to have another go at your ex-wife?"

He smiled again. *"Go?"* he said.

"Scare her," I said. "Intimidate her. You know what they say. Once a sick bastard, always a sick bastard."

"You think I am doing something like that out there from in *here*?" he said. "How could even a brilliant man like myself accomplish such a thing?"

"As I remember it," I said, "you did have a way of being quite persuasive, at least when you weren't drugging women as a way of trying to get into their pants."

"Ancient history," he said. "I have obviously had ample time to work through my issues, as a way of becoming my best self."

"You don't *have* a best self," I said.

He shrugged.

"Do snakes feel that way about themselves

53

when they shed their skin?" I said.

"We're getting stuck here, something I often used to tell my patients," he said. "Is there some specific offense of which you think I am guilty? I'd be fascinated to hear which one. My life in prison is an open book, if not one of Melanie Joan's. Mail is monitored. Emails. Phone calls. There is simply no way for me to get anyone on the outside to do harm to Melanie Joan, someone for whom I still have genuine affection, as hard as that might be for you to believe."

"Cell phones are frequently smuggled into prison," I said, "and passed around. Arrangements can certainly be made, especially by a clever boy like you, John."

Now he waited. Two could play that game. But he still didn't do well with silence. My own therapist, Dr. Susan Silverman, could wait out a glacier.

"Now, I *will* admit," he said, "that there were times, earlier in my incarceration, when I did hold on to, shall we say, certain old fantasies, until I realized they were just holding me back."

"Care to say which ones?"

"Revenge, of course," he said. "Against her. Against you. Even against your resourceful ex-husband."

He made a gesture as if releasing a bird

from the palm of his hand.

"But I've let them go," he said, almost proudly.

He smiled again. "I'm even treating other patients, if unofficially."

I said, "I see a future spike in recidivism on the horizon."

"Did you come all this way to insult me," he said, "or get the questions you have about me answered?"

"What, I can't do both?"

"As much as I would love to flatter myself and think I still have my old power over dear Melanie Joan," he said, "I have nothing to do with her any longer. My world is here within these walls, for now. And I think we're done here."

"Before you go," I said, "I was wondering why you didn't think the letter you sent to Melanie Joan a few months ago, about how the two of you would meet again someday, was worth mentioning."

He seemed genuinely surprised. Or maybe this was just one more pose.

"I wasn't being serious."

"She says you sure sounded serious."

"Well," he said, "she does lie, you know, when it suits her."

Melvin had me there. He abruptly stood up now, took a few steps toward the door, then turned around and came back.

"I forgot to ask," he said, "about what Melanie Joan's current problems actually are. Would *you* care to share?"

"Not so much."

He titled his head to the side, his face looking quizzical.

"I mean, what's going on with the old girl?" he said. "Somebody accusing her of stealing or something?"

There was something flickering in his eyes now. A snake indeed.

"Anyway, nice to see you, Sunny," he said. "Even under these circumstances." He paused and smiled one last time. "Please tell your ex-husband how pleased I am that his son has turned into a handsome young man."

I stared at him.

"Oh, and one more thing," he said. "Sorry that things didn't work out for you and Chief Stone."

Mic drop.

Then he was out the door.

NINE

Richie and I were walking Rosie the dog up Chestnut Street and into Beacon Hill proper. It was two in the afternoon. His son Richard was in school for another hour. I'd told him first thing what Melvin had said about Richard. Richie Burke had suggested his own contact visit with John Melvin, as a way of getting into a room with him.

"He's bluffing," I said.

"I'm glad you pointed that out," Richie said.

"Ever vigilant," I said.

"Makes two of us."

By now we had changed the subject. I'd asked about his other ex-wife, Kathryn, and was informed she was currently in a new period of self-discovery, this time in Taos.

"Isn't she eventually going to run out of selves to discover?" I asked.

"You never run out of those Brit TV shows with the horny vicars," Richie said.

57

"They're not horny," I said. "They're just star-crossed."

"Like us," Richie said.

"I think of us more as stars that intermittently *un*cross," I said.

He was holding Rosie's leash. He didn't love this Rosie the way he had the original. But she didn't know that. If she did, she didn't let on.

"There's nothing stopping us," he said.

"Other than me," I said. "Who at this point in the proceedings would prefer to discuss other things."

"How come you always get to set the terms of the engagement?" Richie said.

I smiled.

"I'm the girl," I said.

He said okay, he'd drop the subject, and asked how Spike was doing on his first day watching Melanie Joan.

"She did some press around town," I said. "He was with her at every stop, without incident. He actually gets a kick out of her."

"When is she moving in?"

"Later this afternoon," I said. "Although reluctantly."

"I assume you're not letting her check out of the hotel."

"We're going to sneak her out a side entrance, the one that faces the Public Alley," I said. "Spike will be waiting in his car. The bags will follow her later. Lots and lots of bags."

"Sounds like a good play to me," he said. "Safe rather than sorry."

"It's only temporary. And if anybody tries anything at the house, I'll be there. And the game will officially be afoot."

"If you need more backup," Richie said, "you know I can supply it."

"Spike and I have this for now," I said.

"You and Spike," he said. "Two stars who are always aligned. Makes me jealous of things being so easy between the two of you and so complicated with us."

I gave him a quick, sisterly peck on the cheek.

"No offense," I said. "But I do look at Spike as being pretty much the perfect man."

"He's gay," Richie said.

"What's your point?" I said.

TEN

We ate dinner at 4 River Street Place. Formerly Melanie Joan's home. Now mine. I insisted that she take the master bedroom. She out-insisted me and took the guest bedroom on the second floor, which, I had to admit, wasn't like moving into the Y.

Spike cooked. It was our shared and dirty little secret that he was a much better chef than the one he employed at his restaurant. He had gone to DeLuca's Market on Charles and come back with the proper fixings for gemelli pasta with chicken sausage and broccoli rabe, Caesar salad with fried oysters on top, fingerling potatoes. When I told Melanie Joan that Spike was a better chef than his employee, he told me to stop it.

"Do you really want me to?" I said.

"God, no," he said. "Don't stop . . . believing . . ."

Just like that he was singing. It happened

60

that way a lot.

"Is there any way to stop you from bursting into song?" I said.

"There is," he said. "But it's really *really* hard."

We sat in the dining room on the first floor I rarely used. Spike, being Spike, did most of the talking. Normally that would have been no small thing in Melanie Joan's presence, like being in there with the champ. But she was remarkably subdued tonight, at least for her. She did talk about her day, and shared that one of the male hosts had hit on Spike before Melanie had politely informed him that Spike was otherwise engaged at the moment.

"But before we left," she said, "I did tell him to keep hope alive."

Before long Melanie Joan was wondering when she might return to The Newbury. I told her on her next trip to Boston. I quoted Jesse Stone, something I still did a lot, unable to help myself, on how being overly cautious never got anybody killed.

"Do you honestly believe my life is in danger?" Melanie Joan asked me.

"No," I said. "But that doesn't mean it's not."

Spike poured more wine for everybody.

"Will somebody be watching this house?"

Melanie Joan said.

"Yes," I said. "I will."

It occurred to me that she seemed less blond than she used to be, and of course less lined. It made me think of the old Indiana Jones line, about how it wasn't the years, it was the mileage. In Melanie Joan's case, it wasn't so much the years as the maintenance.

I had read a line once, I forgot where, about the mask becoming the man. In all ways, physical and not, the mask had become the woman seated across from me.

She sipped some wine, and seemed suddenly, and quietly, lost in thought.

Finally she said, "How did John look?"

"I told you," I said. "As old as the Cryptkeeper."

"Did he ask about me?" she said.

The same faraway look in her eyes.

"It really wasn't that kind of conversation," I said.

"What kind of conversation was it, if I might ask," she said, "if the subject wasn't me?"

"And the object, too!" Spike said brightly.

Melanie Joan stared at him as if he'd just said something in Farsi.

"I wasn't there to catch up with the son of a bitch," I said. "I was there to get a sense

62

as to whether or not he might be looking to get even with you for putting him there."

"I didn't do anything to the son of a bitch other than marry him," she said.

"He's sick," I said.

"Well," she said, "he wasn't always."

"Be that as it may," I said.

"Tell me again how he looked," she said, undeterred.

"You mean, did he look like someone who could have written you a threatening email to follow up on a threatening letter?" I said. "Hell, yes."

"But you said he denied it," Melanie Joan said.

"I'm sorry, Melanie Joan," I said, "but are you acting as a prosecutor here or defense attorney?"

"There's no need to be mean," she said.

"If it's any consolation," Spike said, "she can do meaner."

"He really looked that old?" Melanie Joan said.

Like trying to take a bone away from a dog, I thought.

"Like he's aged thirty years," I said.

"Well, now," she said, suddenly brightening herself. "Then it's not as if the visit was a total loss."

Spike turned to me. "Do you really think

he could be behind this?"

"He's only the first person I've talked to," I said. "For now, let's call him a person of interest."

"Let's," Spike said.

We'd finished the wine, and dinner, by then. Spike was already hinting about some secret dessert he'd hidden in the refrigerator.

"Melanie Joan," I said, "before Spike and I clear the table, there's something I need to ask you."

"How could I say no to my guardian angel?" she said.

"Well," Spike said, "maybe the guardian part."

"Is there someone in your past," I said to her, "who might have reason to believe, even incorrectly, that he or she once had an idea for Cassandra Demeter similar to your own?"

"How dare you even ask me that?" she said.

Going for indignant. But coming up well short, I felt.

"You're sure?"

"I am *not* the person of interest here," she said. "My God, Sunny, you can be impertinent sometimes, when you're not being downright rude."

Spike grinned.

"She swears she's trying to quit," he said to Melanie Joan. "But I frankly feel she's full of shit."

Melanie Joan's phone, on the table next to her plate, suddenly played the first few bars of the *Gone With the Wind* theme.

She turned the phone over, looked at the screen, said, "Excuse me, I need to take this."

She pushed her chair back and got up and walked toward the back of the house, keeping her voice low. Spike and I began clearing the table while we waited for her to come back.

She didn't.

I finally called out to her. No answer. She wasn't in the kitchen and wasn't in her room.

Wasn't anywhere in the house.

"You think it was something we said?" I said.

"Some guardian angel you are," he said.

"Look who's talking."

ELEVEN

Spike and I had searched the neighborhood once we realized she was gone. I had called Samantha Heller and asked if she had the ability to track Melanie Joan's location on her phone. She said that sadly she did not; Melanie Joan wouldn't allow it, that she refused to be treated like some teenager whose mommy and daddy wanted to know her whereabouts at all times of the day or night.

We called the bar at The Newbury, then called the front desk and asked them to check her room, on the chance that she'd gone back there. Maybe she had planned to slip out all along, and was just waiting for the call. Maybe she had called a cab. Or an Uber. She must have left her bag, with her purse in it, in the kitchen, because she hadn't brought it to the dinner table. And now it was gone.

"Fired up," Spike said. "Ready to go."

"Without even waiting to see what you made for dessert," I said.

Spike finally left. He had spent the day with her. The reason he had spent the day with her was that we had determined that she might be in danger. Then she had snuck out the first chance she got, *like* a teenage girl trying to get away from Mommy and Daddy.

I periodically tried her phone, but it went straight to voicemail. Maybe when she came back, I'd find a way to sync up Find my Friends on our phones, as extremely unfriendly as I was feeling toward her at the moment.

Rosie and I took our last walk at around midnight, so she could perform her nightly oblations.

I was reading The *Globe* around eight the next morning when I heard the front door. I had given Melanie Joan her own key. The only other person with one was Spike, and I knew he was at home, because he'd just called wanting to know if she'd shown up yet.

Then there she was, in the same clothes she'd been wearing when she slipped out, plum-colored jeans that were a size too small for her figure, black sweater, sandals I knew were Manolo. Doing what was once known as the walk of shame, before even thinking something like that would get you drummed out of the feminist movement. *Walk of shame?* Just one more thing that made me feel as old as the Old State House.

I briefly wondered how she'd play it, but didn't have to wait long to find out.

She just went for pushy broad, another one of her specialties.

"You are *not* allowed to be cross with me," she said.

She tossed her own Prada bag on the kitchen counter and proceeded to make herself a cup of coffee from my Keurig. When she sat down across from me she said, "Well, aren't you going to say something?"

"Sure," I said. "I quit."

TWELVE

I'd gotten up, walked past her and out of the room, on my way to walking right out of the house. It was still hers, of course. The house. But Rosie and I had been there a long time. And Melanie Joan wasn't the only one who could act like a drama queen.

"Where are you going?" she called after me.

"Walking to work," I said. "Just no longer working for you."

I don't know how she managed to get into her sneakers as fast as she did, but she caught up to me when I was about to cross Beacon and head into the park. She was out of breath.

"You can't quit," she said.

"Watch me," I said. "Rosie and I can be packed up and out by tomorrow."

"Why are you acting this way?"

Now she sounded like a petulant child, which, in so many ways, she was.

"I'm not acting any way," I said. "Well, maybe a little anxious. I get that way sometimes when I'm between clients."

"But *I'm* your client," she said.

"Were," I said. "You're the writer, Melanie Joan. Keep your tenses straight."

I was walking briskly as we passed the duckling statues in the Public Garden, just a few yards from Beacon. She was keeping up with me. Maybe this would be her morning walk today. We angled to the left then, toward Charles, where we had to wait for the light to cross. This wasn't the most direct route to my office, but I liked walking past the playground set in the far corner of the Boston Common where my father used to take me when I was little.

"How can I make things right between us?" Melanie Joan said now. "I can't lose you."

"You can start by telling me where you were last night," I said. "And who you were with."

She huffed. "Well, if you must know, I was with a man," she said.

"What man?"

"It doesn't matter."

"Humor me."

"I can't tell you," she said.

"And why is that?"

"Because he's married!"

The force of the way she said it almost made me laugh.

"I don't care!" I said.

We stopped briefly at the playground. It was early, but there were a lot of parents and children here already, on one of those Boston mornings that made the rest of the world feel like out of town. I watched a dad help his daughter across the monkey bars.

"Is there a reason why we're standing here?" she said.

"Because I like it here," I said.

"Oh," she said.

"Back to your mystery man," I said as we headed for Boylston.

"I promised him I wouldn't tell," Melanie Joan said.

"I can keep a secret," I said. "You can look it up, it's right there in the code of conduct for private detectives."

"Are you sure?"

"It's one of the things that keeps me young," I said, adding, "though not everyone seems to think so these days."

We were passing the little store in Park Plaza that actually still had a KENO sign in the window, and then The Trolley Shop. There was no one around us, but Melanie Joan lowered her voice.

"It's my manager," she said.

"Oh, ho," I said. I turned my head and grinned at her. "Richard Gross, you dog, you."

"Very funny," she said.

"Not so much."

She said, "Richard took the early flight from Los Angeles yesterday."

"And you didn't think you could trust Spike or me to know you'd gone off for a night of carnal passion at your cutie's hotel?" I said.

If she appreciated me trying to sound like one of her novels, she hid it well. But then irony had never been one of Melanie Joan Hall's strong suits, for as long as I had known her.

"Richard is here because he wants to take charge of my current situation," she said. "I stuck up for you and told him you were in charge. And now this is the thanks I get."

"How can I be such an ungrateful bitch?" I said. "Whatever gets into me?"

She solemnly shook her head in agreement. That was it for irony this morning. Maybe the whole rest of the week.

"Where is Spike?" she said.

"I told him he could take the day off."

"But who's going to watch me when you're not around?"

"I'm sure Richard Gross will think of something," I said. "It sounds like he knows everything."

"But I want you and Spike," she said.

"Then you need to act like it," I said. "It's rather difficult for Spike and me to protect you if we don't know where you are."

We had walked up the stairs and were in my office. I sat down behind my desk and called Spike and told him our wayward girl had come home. Melanie Joan made a face. I called Samantha Heller after I hung up with Spike. She asked if I needed anything. I told her she could email me Melanie Joan's schedule for the day, which she did.

Spike was with us in the office a half-hour later, telling Melanie Joan he would drive her back to River Street Place. She had decided to do a book signing while she was in Boston. She said it was for fun. I knew it was for an ego stroke. She was due at the Barnes & Noble at the Prudential Center at eleven. It gave her plenty of time for the essentials. Hair, makeup, wardrobe.

I asked Spike if he would walk Rosie while Melanie Joan was getting ready.

"I'm starting to feel like your concierge," he said.

"I'm a big tipper," I said.

"Since when?" Spike said.

Once they were gone I was happily alone behind the rustic wood desk that I loved, enjoying some Melanie Joan–free time, amazed at how quickly time away from her had become this meaningful. But reminding myself once more how much Rosie and I owed her. And as crazy as it was, and as crazy as I knew she was, I did like her.

I was checking emails, finding even that task enjoyable today, when my father called.

"Busy?" he said.

"Never too busy for my pops," I said.

"I have a problem I need to discuss with you," he said.

"What kind?"

"A Joe Doyle problem," he said.

The most powerful lawyer in Boston, as bad as the bad guys he so often defended. And one with whom my father had history, none good.

"The one and only," I said.

"Himself," Phil Randall said.

"Can you briefly describe the problem?" I said.

"I think he might want to kill me," my father said.

74

THIRTEEN

Rita Fiore, red-haired she-devil, might be the best lawyer in Boston, as reluctant as I was to admit it to myself.

But if Rita was the best, Joe Doyle of Doyle and O'Meara truly was still the most powerful and most feared. By my count the only Mob guy he hadn't defended was Richie's father, Desmond, and that was only because Desmond Burke had always been cagey enough and elusive enough never to be arrested for anything, including jaywalking. But if it had ever looked as though Desmond might go down, I was certain his first phone call would have been to Doyle.

Joe Doyle didn't discriminate. MeToo guys formally charged with sexual assault. Men and women up to their eyeballs with SEC trouble, which simply meant a different class of gangster. And an assortment of people, over time, who had been charged with murder in the Commonwealth of Massachusetts. He didn't get them all off. But my count, he kept more out of jail than not.

But he hadn't been able to save Joe Jr. from Phil Randall.

The problem for Joe Doyle Jr. was that he had aspired to only one big thing: growing up to be the kind of thug his father might someday have to defend in court. He first began to build a thriving business for opioids when he was still at Harvard, and had grown it into a small local empire.

"A combination of daddy issues," my own daddy had once said, "and being a rich, entitled punk."

As the market for painkillers exploded, things had gone well for Joe Doyle Jr. until my father, in one of his last acts as a truly great detective for the BPD, had arrested him for being the point man in a criminal conspiracy. It resulted in the death of a rival drug kingpin — I'd often wondered how many queenpins there might be out there — found floating in the Swan Boats pond at the Public Garden.

It took years of appeals and a lot of behind-the-scenes arm-twisting from Joe Jr.'s father for the kid's case to grind its way through the system. But the son had finally ended up as a permanent guest of the state at MCI-Concord, doing twenty-five-to-life.

That was until somebody shanked him in the prison yard about ten days ago.

Joe Doyle Jr., around my age as I recalled, had proclaimed his innocence to the end, claiming that he had been set up. At the time of his death his father had just mounted another appeal, based on what he said was new evidence.

Evidence he said that Detective Phil Randall had ignored, because of what Doyle described as a vendetta.

"Only if *vendetta* means getting the guy who did it," my father said.

The death of Joe Doyle Jr. had been big news for a couple days. But once it was out of *The Globe* and largely off social media and television, I assumed that the story had played itself out.

I was about to find out how wrong I had been about that.

I met my father at the French Press Bakery & Café in Needham, twenty minutes or so from the house in which I had grown up. We sat at a long window table. I knew from experience he would tell me what had happened at his own speed. And he did, first telling me that he was certain he'd seen Joe Doyle watching us the night we'd been at The Street Bar, but hadn't wanted to worry me.

Then when he was walking to the lot where he'd parked the car on Newbury, he thought he noticed two men following him. When he let them know that he'd spotted them, they turned and walked away toward Commonwealth. But when he got to the corner of Comm Ave. and Dartmouth, they were gone.

"Maybe I've lost a step," he said.

"Unlikely," I said.

"Happens."

"Are we getting anywhere near the part where Joe Doyle threatened to kill you?"

"Are you going to let me tell this?" he said.

This morning, after he did his morning walk on the track at Newton High School and was on his way to his car, Doyle had stepped out of a black Lincoln SUV. With him were the same two men my father had spotted after he'd left The Newbury that night.

The conversation was brief. According to my father, Doyle began by asking him if he was a religious man. My father said he was, not that it was any of Doyle's business. Then Doyle asked if he was familiar with the twenty-fourth chapter of Leviticus, and my father said he was not.

My father handed me his phone then. He'd taken a snapshot of the relevant pas-

78

sage in his own Bible when he'd gotten home.

I read out loud. " 'If anyone injures his neighbor, whatever he has done must be done to him. Fracture for fracture, eye for eye, tooth for tooth. As he has injured another, so must he be injured.' "

I started to hand my father his phone back when he said, "Read all the way to the end."

" 'Whoever kills a man must be put to death.' "

"Doyle quoted it to you," I said.

"He certainly did."

I slid the phone across the table to him.

"I told him that I didn't kill his son," Phil Randall said. "And Doyle said, 'You might as well have. And now you need to pay for that.' "

"Pay how, exactly?" my father had said.

And Doyle had said, "What part of an eye for an eye didn't you understand, Detective?"

Then he got back into the SUV, which drove away.

"He's an officer of the court," I said. "You need to report him."

"For what? Quoting the Old Testament?"

"It's like you're one of his witnesses he's trying to intimidate," I said.

"I picked up on that fact myself," my

father said.

He'd ordered two blueberry muffins. It was an implied-type thing that they were both for him. The only things left now on our plates were crumbs. At least Joe Doyle hadn't adversely affected his appetite. But from experience I knew hardly anything could.

"Maybe you and Mom should get away for a few days," I said. "Or more than a few."

"I don't run," he said. "From entitled punks of any age."

"Had to give it a shot," I said.

"Mr. Doyle and me, we're about the same age," he said. "He doesn't want to spend the rest of his days behind bars because he had me killed the way his kid killed that bum."

"Maybe he doesn't think that way," I said. "Man's got a lot of friends in low places."

My father said, "You make a good point."

"Tony Marcus told me one time that the best way to act on a grudge is to wait," I said.

"Speaking of friends in low places."

"I could pull Spike off Melanie Joan," I said.

Phil Randall said, "She's a paying client."

"Ish," I said.

Suddenly we were the only customers in

the place. My father went quiet now, staring past me and out the window. He had always been as confident, in his own quiet way, as anybody I had ever known, and as comfortable in his own skin. Like Richie that way. And Jesse Stone, too. I could hear the voice of Dr. Susan Silverman inside my head, asking me if I could detect any sort of pattern.

"Maybe I could go to see him," my father said.

"You could," I said, "but you're not going to. At this point, poking the bear would only escalate the situation, not that you asked."

"I didn't ask."

"Didn't have to."

"I hate not knowing," Phil Randall said.

"I know the feeling."

"Inherited trait," he said.

"One of many," I said. "Starting with stubbornness."

"Tell me about it."

I sipped cold coffee.

"He's not being reasonable," I said.

"You think?"

"His son did what you arrested him for doing. And it wasn't you who found him guilty. As I recall, a jury did."

"But in his mind, it's like I'm the one who handed whoever killed him the knife," Phil Randall said. "Then he got done the way

Leo Morales did."

The rival drug dealer whose people, I was certain, had somehow managed to eye-for-an-eye Joe Doyle Jr. in the prison yard.

"I need to find a way to keep you and Mom safe," I said.

"I've always been able to look out for myself," my father said.

"Dad," I said, "you wouldn't have called if you didn't want my help. So let me help."

He smiled again, as if trying not to look like what I knew he was at this moment, even if I'd never say that to him, and he'd never admit it to me:

A frightened old man.

"Help how?" he asked.

"I actually have an idea," I said.

"One I bet I'm going to hate."

"Possibly even more," I said, "than you've always hated the Yankees."

FOURTEEN

While Spike and Melanie Joan dined together at Spike's, I drove to Charlestown.

"Where are you going?" Melanie Joan asked before I left the house.

Somehow our détente had lasted until the dinner hour. But the night was young.

"To see a gangster," I said.

"May I ask which one?" she said.

"Mine," I said.

My former father-in-law, Desmond Burke, lived at Flagship Wharf, part of the old Navy Yard in Charlestown. From his house you could see the Bunker Hill monument as well as the USS *Constitution.* The movie *Married to the Mob* had come out long before I married Richie Burke. But the facts, insofar as I knew them, were that Richie had never been a participant in the family business with his father and his uncles. It didn't change the fact that I had been a member of a Mob family at one point in my life.

My father had opposed the union, rather strenuously, as fond as he became of Richie over time, and as fond of him as he remained after the union dissolved. But with Phil Randall it had never been about Richie and was all about Desmond, whom he had never managed to arrest. In so many ways, Desmond Burke had been his white whale. And likely always would be.

And if he had even a whiff that I was going to ask Desmond Burke, his nemesis, to help keep him safe from Joe Doyle, it would have made Phil Randall's head spontaneously combust.

And yet here I was.

Desmond Burke was as thin as a knife, hair completely white, the tough Irish kid up from the streets still clinging to power, even outlasting Whitey Bulger, another Boston hoodlum who ended up getting killed in prison. Even the elderly Desmond Burke was still dangerous enough, and everyone in town knew it. But he looked even older than *his* years now, wounded by time and by loss. His brother Felix was gone. So was his brother Peter. Desmond had recently been betrayed, a case in which I was involved, by one of his troopers, in what turned out to be an ambitious but doomed grift. When it ended, I didn't turn

Jalen Washington, the trooper, in to the authorities. I handed him back over to Desmond Burke. There was no need for me to ask what had happened to him, simply because I knew the code of street justice that had always informed Desmond's business, especially when it involved betrayal.

Tonight he was wearing a heavy shawl cardigan, despite the time of year. He had already had his dinner by the time I arrived, and had what I knew was Midleton Very Rare in the glass next to him. He offered me a glass of my own. I accepted.

Two of his men had been stationed in front of the house. I didn't recognize either, but it had been a while since I'd paid a visit to Flagship Wharf.

He had a fire going. It was as if what was left of his life was one long winter, even with Richie's son, Desmond's grandson, now fully back in that life in such a meaningful and, for the old man, happy-making way.

"I sometimes feel as if I only see you when you have run out of other options," he said.

"Not true," I said. "You know how fond I am of you, Desmond."

"And I you," he said. "And not only because you once saved my life."

Another old case.

"Richie and I saved your life," I said.

"You and my son make a good team," he said. "You should still be together."

His voice was as low and harsh-sounding as ever. It was his brother Felix who had been a boxer as a young man. But Desmond sounded as if he was the one who had taken too many punches to the throat.

"You sound like *my* father now," I said.

"Somehow," he said, "I doubt that."

I smiled at him. He nearly smiled back. He raised his glass and I raised mine.

"Slainte," he said.

"Slainte agatsa," I said in response.

To my health, and his.

"So now that we are still in agreement about our affection for each other," he said, "tell me what you need."

I told him about Joe Doyle.

"That prick," Desmond Burke said.

I smiled again and told him we could agree to agree on that.

"His boy died in a box," he said, "and now it sounds to me as if the father wants to put your copper father into a different kind of box."

Copper. An old man from another time reaching back for an expression from that time.

"I'm hoping that as a favor to me," I said, "you can have a couple of your men watch my father until I can figure out a way to make Joe Doyle back the hell off."

He shook his head.

"Men like Doyle don't do that," he said. "It is all about face with them, a hard world in which they only see two options. Looking strong or looking weak. Nothing in between."

"He's being irrational, blaming my father for his son's death," I said.

"Old men often *are* irrational," he said, "when they are looking to settle old scores."

He drank some Midleton.

"I could talk to him," he said.

"I plan to talk to him first," I said.

"Of course," Desmond said.

Now I drank. The whiskey went down smoothly. An old and familiar feeling. I imagined it making its way through my system, every part of it, like warm running water.

"Can you do this for me?" I said.

"Yes," he said. "And no."

"Not sure I understand."

"Yes," he said, "I will do this because it is you asking me to do it. In my mind, you are still my son's wife."

"Ex."

"Not to me," he said. "And certainly not to him."

Nothing for me to say there, so I just waited for him to explain himself.

"There is just one condition," he said finally.

I waited again.

"Your copper father comes here and asks me himself," he said.

"Let me talk to him about that," I said.

"Do," Desmond Burke said.

But that conversation, as uncomfortable as it would be for my father and me, would have to wait, as it turned out. Because it was right about that same time, I would find out later, that Phil Randall's car was being sideswiped on Storrow Drive.

FIFTEEN

He'd already been stitched and released at Mass General, only a few minutes away from where the accident occurred, by the time he called and told me what had happened and asked me to come pick him up.

My father described it as an "accident that wasn't really an accident."

"You're saying somebody tried to run you off the road intentionally?" I said.

"Let's just say that whoever it was didn't do very much to keep me *on* the road," Phil Randall said.

"Are you okay, Dad?" I said.

"Better than my poor little Jetta," he said.

I picked him up at the emergency room entrance on Fruit Street. If he was scared, or even shaken, about what had happened, he wasn't going to let on to me. Old habits. When I got out and came around to the passenger side, he waved me away.

"I can get into the car on my own, driver,"

he said, and winked.

The small butterfly bandage was on the left side of his forehead. I asked how many stitches. "Four too many," he said.

It had happened, he said, at the end of Storrow, where you got off for the North End. He had been on his way to meet an old cop friend for a Celtics playoff game.

"You think this was Doyle's doing?" I said.

"Probably no way of knowing that for sure," he said.

"Don't *be* so sure," I said.

The last time I had rushed to the emergency room at Mass General was when Richie had been shot a few years earlier. The shooter was just delivering a message that night. Perhaps the same thing had happened to my father. Except my father was an aging man who I didn't even want driving at night anymore, who could have been killed.

"Have you told Mom?" I said.

"I have not," he said. "She still thinks I'm at the game."

"What are you *going* to tell Mom?" I said.

"I am going to tell her that someone ran a red light," he said. "And you're going to back that version of things until the cows come home."

"Let me take *you* home," I said.

"After a whiskey at yours first," he said.

Irish whiskey with my father and my former father-in-law on the same night, I thought. Sunny and the boys. Just sunshine boys in this case.

Spike was watching an Ultimate Fighting event in the living room. He said it was pay-per-view, but knew I wouldn't have wanted him to miss it. Melanie Joan, whom he said had been slightly overserved at Spike's, had long since gone up to bed.

My father was behind me when we came through the front door. When Spike saw him, he shut off the television. After hearing what had happened, he said, "We need to pay a visit to Mr. Doyle, I'm thinking. Like first thing."

"And tell him what?" my father said. "That my car got hit by another car in the North End? The bastard is probably looking for a reaction, but I'll be damned if I'm going to give him one."

I went and poured Jameson for him and Spike. A small one for me, since I'd already had my fill at Desmond Burke's, and still had to drive my father home. He sat at the end of the couch. Rosie was already curled up next to him. Acting as an emotional therapy dog was just one of her greatest

91

talents, when she wasn't acting like a treat whore.

He described again the exact spot where the accident happened, where you got off on Nashua Street for what was now known as the TD Garden.

"At first I thought it was just some knuckleball trying to get ahead of me," he said.

"We know who the knuckleball is," I said. "At some point we just have to prove it."

"And we will," he said.

I grinned. "Because you're you, and I'm just like you," I said.

"Dog with a bone," he said.

"There must be a better way to describe me."

He drank some of his whiskey and said, "Ahhh."

"It actually could have been worse," he said.

"This has to stop," I said.

"I could put a charge into Doyle," Spike said. He grinned. "With gusto."

"I'm telling you," my father said, "it would only make things worse. And he'd deny he had anything to do with it."

"Until the cows came home," I said.

My father winked at me again and idly scratched Rosie behind one of her ears. He had worn his lucky green Celtics sweater under his blazer. I noticed a few flecks of dried blood on the front. Somehow I had to convince him to accept help from an old Mob guy because a famous Boston lawyer was acting like one.

Just not tonight.

"I think I'm ready to go home, kiddo," my father said.

He had settled deep into the couch with Rosie. But when I tried to help him up, he ignored my hand and said, "I'm fine."

He wasn't. I wasn't. I asked Spike to stay until I got back.

"We'll come up with a plan in the morning," Spike said to both of us.

I was way ahead of him.

SIXTEEN

There had been no further emails or phone calls or messages left at The Newbury for Melanie Joan, so she announced at breakfast the next morning that this needed to be a shopping day, and asked if I wanted to come along because Spike would probably be bored out of his mind on such a trip.

I told her that meant she didn't know Spike nearly as well as she thought she did.

"Are you sure you don't want to come along?" she said.

I told her then what had happened to my father.

"Holy hell," she said. "It sounds like he might be in more danger than I am."

"Last night he was," I said.

"You have an awful lot going on all of a sudden," she said.

I flexed my biceps as a way of showing off all the work with weights I had been doing at Henry Cimoli's gym.

"Boston strong," I said.

Joe Doyle's law offices were in the International Trust Company Building, a landmark Beaux Arts structure on Milk Street built in the late nineteenth century, one that still had figures representing industry and commerce and fidelity carved into the stone between the windows on the second floor. All in all, the old place was still something to see.

Doyle's own office was on the top floor. His assistant, an attractive but severe-looking woman with steel-gray hair, asked if I had an appointment after I showed her my card.

"Only in Samarra," I said.

She stared up at me, trying to look both imperious and vaguely amused at the same time. Her nameplate read *Mary Horgan.*

"Excuse me?" she said.

"Appointment in Samarra," I said. "The O'Hara novel about fate and inevitability."

She smiled now. I smiled back. Mine was way better. I knew I could win a smile-off with her any day of the week.

"Perhaps you could call later and state your business and try to set up an appointment," she said. "As unlikely as that is with Mr. Doyle's schedule."

"But I'm here now," I said. "And I bet

he's here now. Don't you think it would be counterintuitive to postpone fate this way?" I shrugged. "And inevitability?"

"You should leave," she said.

"Nope," I said. "Not leaving. Not calling later. Not happening."

"Do I need to call security?" she said.

By now she'd stopped smiling at me.

"What you need to do," I said, "is tell Joe that Phil Randall's daughter would like to see him, just so we can stop fucking around here, Mary."

SEVENTEEN

"I've heard what a tough guy you think you are," Joe Doyle said. "You should know that I've been tougher a lot longer."

"Thanks for the heads-up."

Doyle said, "I do think you frightened my assistant, however."

"Then she's the one who needs to toughen up," I said.

Joe Doyle was a large man even sitting down, which is how he had remained as Mary, that delicate flower, had shown me in. He had massive hands that fit the rest of him, palms flat on the desk in front of him, nails, I noticed, a-gleamin'. He had a tan he hadn't gotten naturally, after a rainy month of May. Mostly bald, white hair around the fringes. Everything about him neat. Including the desk.

"Why are you bothering me?" he said.

"Why are you bothering my father?" I said. "Or would 'threatening' be a more accurate way of describing it?"

"I didn't threaten him," Doyle said. "Poor Phil must be starting to get a bit wobbly in his old age."

Doyle had a big voice, too. It was described in some of the articles I'd read as "commanding." So he had that going for him. I tried to remain calm in its presence. And his.

"Somebody tried to run his car off the road last night," I said.

I was wearing one of my favorite summer dresses, a Tucker I'd just bought. I crossed my legs. He watched me do it. He was old, too, but clearly not dead.

"This happened to my father not long after you were quoting Leviticus to him," I said, "you son of a bitch."

I saw a slight twitch to his head. Not much, there and gone. He was made of much sturdier stuff than his assistant.

"I hope he's all right," Doyle said.

"You know he is," I said. "Maybe we should stop dicking around here."

He managed to remain calm.

"Maybe you're trying too hard to be tough," he said, "and sound that way."

"I frankly come by it naturally."

I noticed pictures of his son on the bookcase behind him. In one he was wearing a cap and gown, looking a full head smaller than his father.

"Is there a purpose for you barging in on me this way," Doyle said, "with information you say I already had?"

"I want you to leave my father alone," I said. "He's not the one who put your son in jail. The trial did that, as I recall."

"Your father knew my son was innocent," Doyle said.

"He did what he always did," I said. "He followed the evidence."

"For all I care," Doyle said, "he can follow it straight to hell."

"You obviously don't know him as well as you think you do," I said. "God likes my dad best."

He leaned forward slightly.

"Do you honestly think I would risk my good name on some has-been cop?" he said.

"Define 'good name.'"

"We're done here," he said.

"I'm just wondering what your endgame is here, Joe," I said. "How far you plan to take this."

"Assuming that I had something to do with what happened to him last night," he said.

"For the sake of conversation."

"Maybe just this," he said. "Maybe I want

him to realize that there are all sorts of ways of doing time."

He patted his desk with the big hands.

"Now, please get out of my office and don't bother me again," he said.

He stood. Even taller than I had thought. When I stood, I was looking up at him. The desired effect.

"And you might want to remind him that there is no greater pain for a parent than being predeceased by a child."

We both let that settle for a moment.

"Now you're threatening me?" I said.

"Good day, Ms. Randall," he said.

I didn't ask him to define *good* this time as I turned and left his office, thinking this showed all the signs of being an especially shitty week.

About to get worse.

EIGHTEEN

Someone had gotten into my office while I'd been away.

I had never really considered anything in the office worth stealing, with the exception of my laptop, and everything on that was backed up, here and on my Mac at home and on the all-powerful and all-seeing cloud. All of my artwork, other than whatever piece in the office I was working on at the moment — usually when bored waiting for a paying client to walk through the door — was also at the house I still thought of as Melanie Joan's, by sheer force of habit.

I had a file cabinet I didn't really need. Also out of force of habit, an antique from before you could do everything digitally except get your nails done.

I had a decent deadbolt lock on the door, and an alarm system, one I consistently neglected to set. I knew it wouldn't take much for an artist like Ghost Garrity to get past the lock, or the alarm when it was set, and storm the citadel.

But now someone else had managed. I gave a cursory search of the room, and of my desk, and decided that the only thing different from the last time I'd been inside was a small stack of papers on my desk.

Yellow, handwritten pages, slightly faded blue ink, the script like schoolgirl handwriting out of the past.

I liked a neat desk. Despite my line of work, and despite the fact that my personal and professional lives so frequently skewed toward being a bit of a mess, I actually hated chaos.

And clutter.

And I tried to do something about both when I could, if only for the sake of appearances.

"You keep trying to find your inner neat freak," Spike said. "You just never quite get there."

The stack of papers was the only thing on my blotter. No note on top, or on the side. The small framed photographs on my desk exactly where they'd been before.

Just the handwritten pages in the school-girl script were new.

I sat down and counted them. Ten pages in all.

"Chapter One" was on top of the first page, followed in this way:

My name is Athena Mars and this is the beginning of my story, about a life of great adventure. By the end of my story, you might think that what I've told you is the kind of mythology from which my name comes. But I'm not a god, just a girl who wanted the whole world to know her name.

I got up then and walked across the room to the inlaid bookcase that I'd had built, with the permission of my landlord, when I'd leased this space. On the top shelf was a signed first edition of Melanie Joan's break-through debut novel.

The title was *A Girl and Not a God.*

It was the book that began with Cassandra Demeter sharing, in the first person, that she was about to tell us about love and heartbreak. And about a life of great adventure. That was how Melanie Joan's prologue started, about a girl who said *her* name came out of mythology, who said she wanted the whole world to know her name.

Okay, I thought, *so maybe this was a first draft of Melanie Joan's, somehow recaptured from the way-back machine.*

Now I flipped back to the title and author

page, where she had inscribed the book to me:

"To Sunny. One in a million. MJ."

I carried the book across the room, sat back down at my desk, opened the book again to the inscription, and laid it next to the pages in front of me.

Not the same handwriting.

Maybe a first draft, but not Melanie Joan Hall's.

"Oh, ho," I said.

NINETEEN

Because of the early hour I made myself a cup of strong coffee, not the strong drink I would have preferred at the moment.

First I read the handwritten pages of the manuscript. Then compared it to the flowery prose of Melanie Joan Hall. Neither work was great literature. But I felt that the anonymous pages that had been left for me were better, less overwritten. Much easier to read than *A Girl and Not a God.*

But the beginning of the manuscript was, at the very least, the beginning of the same story, set in Boston, turn of the twentieth century. The names were different. Much of the dialogue was different. But Athena Mars was Cassandra Demeter. Our Dickensian heroines were giving us basically the same introduction to their up-from-the-bootstraps beginnings.

Hundred percent.

I called Spike and asked him where he and

Melanie Joan were.

"Zegna," he said. "Copley Place Mall."

"I know where Zegna is."

"I'm almost embarrassed to tell you that she wants to buy me a jacket."

"No way."

"Way."

"I meant no way you're embarrassed."

"So strong," he said. "And yet so weak sometimes."

I asked when he expected to have her back at the house. He said soon.

"Shopping is a lot like sports," Spike said. "Her legs just finally gave out."

I was waiting for them when they returned to River Street Place. Spike carried most of the shopping bags, some from Newbury Street, some from the high-end stores at the mall. Melanie Joan carried a couple herself, one from Fendi, one from Christian Louboutin. It had been their first shopping date. I was worried that next they'd want to go to the aquarium.

"We need to talk," I said to Melanie Joan.

The pages were now in the middle of my coffee table. She hadn't yet noticed them, still in a post-shopping glow.

"Well, that sounds serious," she said.

"Kind of."

"Do I have time for a glass of wine first?"

"You decide," I said as I handed her the pages. She squinted at them.

"I need my reading glasses," she said.

She reached into her purse for her over-sized reading glasses with the thick black frames, then plopped down on the couch and began to read, stopping after the second page.

"This is someone trying to copy me," she said. "And not doing a very good job of it."

"Okay," I said. "Let's go with that."

She tossed the pages back on the coffee table.

"Who wrote this dreck?" she said.

I said, "I was hoping you might be able to tell me."

"And why is that?" she said.

"Because if the person who wrote this isn't copying you," I said, "then a cynical person might think you copied them."

Our exchange devolved from there.

TWENTY

"I'm curious about something, Ms. Randall," Richard Gross said.

Gross had arrived about half an hour later, Melanie Joan having taken a break from screaming at me for accusing her of being a plagiarist to call him. Then she'd huffed her way upstairs to make herself more presentable for Richard Gross.

I wasn't sure what I had expected the great and powerful Richard Gross to look like. But the rather legendary Hollywood power broker, one who had begun his career Out There as a lawyer, looked more like an actor, reminding me somewhat of Michael Douglas. Not the *Romancing the Stone* Michael Douglas. The older one from Netflix. Long silver hair, toffee-colored tan, not much taller than I was, trim-skinny, killer eyes that were so blue I suspected contact lenses. Not many more lines in his face than Melanie Joan had. Maybe they used the same nip/tucker.

Samantha Heller was also in the living room with us. I had called her while Melanie Joan was upstairs primping. When Samantha arrived, I lied to both Melanie Joan and Richard Gross, saying that I had previously invited Samantha over for a drink today.

I wasn't worried about getting rolled by a Hollywood hotshot like Gross, but I decided I could use a little backup in getting Melanie Joan calmed down, especially after Spike had left for work.

Rosie immediately took to Samantha. Growled at Gross. *Good girl,* I thought.

Gross and Melanie Joan were on the couch. Samantha and I were in the surprisingly comfy antique chairs that had come with the house, on the other side of the coffee table I'd recently purchased.

Gross, I noticed, had a proprietary hand on Melanie Joan Hall's knee, occasionally patting it. Like he wanted *her* to be the good girl. He had already spent a fair amount of time telling me I was pretty much the opposite for upsetting Melanie Joan this way.

"I'll need to take those pages with me when I leave," he said. "By tomorrow I'll have hired the best forensics firm in Boston."

"No," I said.

"Excuse me?" Gross said.

My answer seemed to startle him, as if he had been ready to move on to his next statement. Or perhaps *no* just confused him.

"No," I said, "you can't take the pages. Examining them is my job."

"Sunny's right," Samantha Heller said. "We all need to let her do her job."

"By attacking my character?" Melanie Joan said.

"By trying to get at the truth," Samantha said patiently.

"Whose side are you on?" Melanie Joan said.

"The same side I'm always on," Samantha said to her. "Yours."

Samantha and Gross had barely spoken to each other. But the dislike they so obviously shared for each other, bordering on contempt, made me think of atmospheric electricity. Just not in any kind of positive way.

"Melanie Joan may have hired Ms. Randall here as an investigator," Gross said. "But I am now overseeing her brand, something that involves so much more than her books, Samantha." He looked at Melanie Joan and smiled. "This lady is so much more than an author now. She's an industry."

"An industry that starts with her books," Samantha said.

"And now someone wants to give the impression that the books and the industry both began with plagiarism, Mr. Gross," I said.

"Call me Richard," he said.

There was, I decided in the moment, no reason to tell him that I'd happily been considering calling him "Dick."

"Now this person, whoever it is, is even manufacturing evidence against me!" Melanie Joan said.

Gross patted her knee and turned slightly, so he was more fully facing me.

"Not to make too fine a point of things," Gross said, "but my understanding is that Melanie Joan hired you to find out who is harassing her and not to harass her yourself."

I smiled.

"*I'm* harassing her?" I said. "I'm going to have to call bullshit on that one, Mr. Gross. You know that's not what I did, or am doing. So does Melanie Joan. And Samantha. And people in outer space if they can hear us. What I am trying to find out right now is if Melanie Joan has any idea where this document might have come from. Or from whom."

I held my smile.

"Is all," I said.

"We know you're the victim, Melanie Joan," Samantha Heller said. "Sunny's just looking for some cooperation here. So she *can* do her job."

"I understand that," Melanie Joan said. "I'm not an idiot. But what I will not do is sit here and allow Sunny, as fond as I am of her, to insult me."

"That is not my intent," I said. "But somebody broke into my office because he or she wanted me to see these pages. And wanted you to see them, and perhaps other pages that will follow. What you really need to understand is that all of this means that you and I are both being watched, Melanie Joan. Your hotel room. My office. If your situation isn't necessarily escalating, it is certainly continuing at a rapid clip."

I shot a quick look at Samantha. She nodded.

"The more I know," I continued, "the more I can do to end this as quickly as possible. That means doing what you hired me to do, which is find out who this person is and then make them go away."

"It's not me who copied somebody else's work!" Melanie Joan said. *"Don't you see? It's the other way around!"*

I told her then, with as much conviction as I could muster, that we all understood that had to be the case. I knew of a place in Boston, I said, where I might be able to have the ink and the paper tested, as a way of possibly determining the age of both, even though I suspected that to be a long shot, at best.

"But what will that prove?" Melanie Joan said.

"Hopefully that whoever wrote this wrote it recently, and not at the time when you were beginning to write *A Girl and Not a God,*" I said. "And that you still might be the victim of a shakedown, or a grift. Or both."

"With all due respect," Gross said, "I still believe my people are better able to handle this sort of authentication in a more efficacious manner than you can."

I looked around the room, as if confused.

"All due respect?" I said. "Here?"

"Now, now," Melanie Joan said. "We're all supposed to be on the same team here."

"You sure about that, MJ?" Samantha Heller said.

"Now, Samantha, you know you and Richard have been getting along much better lately," Melanie Joan said.

Samantha grinned.

"You sure about *that*?" Samantha Heller asked.

I picked up the papers, just to have something to do with my hands.

"You don't know who might have written this?" I said.

"I do not!"

"You're certain of that?" I said.

She gave me a long look. "You know, Sunny," she said, "sometimes I think you don't know me at all."

"You know, Melanie Joan," I said, "can't lie. Sometimes I feel the exact same way."

She stood then and announced that she would be staying with Richard tonight. I told her I couldn't protect her at the Mandarin. Richard Gross, sounding insulted, told me that he was all the protection Melanie Joan needed.

"I'll be in touch," Gross said to me. "I have a solid lead on that email. Or at least my people do."

"Care to share?" I said.

"Need to know," he said.

When they were gone, I said to Samantha Heller, "I know you are far more invested in Melanie Joan Inc. than I am, or ever will be. But she may know more about these pages than she's telling."

"No comment," Samantha said.

"And while I know that we're both on her side," I said, "we at least have to now entertain the notion that she is both a thief and a liar. If we weren't entertaining that notion previously."

"But hoping she's not."

"Back at you."

I offered her the drink I'd lied about having invited her over to have before she left. She declined. I fixed myself a Jameson and watched an episode of *Ted Lasso* I'd already watched because Ted and the gang always managed to lift my spirits. Then I built myself a world-class salad, walked Rosie all the way to Beacon Street and back, made sure to set the alarm here when we were done, went upstairs, washed my face, looked for any new facial lines that I might have acquired, moisturized, and brushed.

Then I got into bed and opened my laptop and began to read again, this time about Melanie Joan Hall's most memorable character:

Herself.

TWENTY-ONE

Melanie Joan Krause had grown up in Oneida, New York. The small town, I happened to know, was famous for Oneida silver and for being the geographic center of New York State. And for a Native American tribe still known as the Oneida Indian Tribe. Old school.

"When I was growing up in Oneida," she once told *Vanity Fair*, "we thought going to the city meant Utica."

She grew up without a father, who her mother told her died before she was born, but turned out to have gone out one night for a pack of cigarettes and never returned. She said she got her love of reading and writing from her mother, an English teacher in the town's Seneca Street School. Melanie Joan Krause graduated from Oneida High School and ended up at little Whitesboro College, in a small town next to Utica. After her mother died, she said she managed to pay her way through school working nights at the *Utica Observer-Dispatch.*

It was then, or so she had always told interviewers and feature writers with quotes that were often the same, word for word, that her dream of being a novelist fully took hold. She had short stories published in a campus literary quarterly. And around her work schedule, she did manage to write her first novel, one that she said died a tragic and lonely death in the bottom drawer of her desk.

"Where it shall remain forevermore," she'd said, again and again. "The only way I can properly describe it is that it was as bad as your worst college haircut."

But then she wrote a second novel after college. *A Girl and Not a God* was published to scathing reviews from mainstream critics and became a runaway, word-of-mouth sensation. Within two weeks, it was No. 1 on the *New York Times* Best Seller List, where it remained, taking on all comers, for the next three months. During the time she said she was writing the novel, she had married one of her former English professors from Whitesboro College, Charles Hall, divorcing him just a year later. But by the time the book became a hit, she was Melanie Joan Hall, and the world knew her name the way Cassandra Demeter, her creation, wanted the world to know hers.

The way Athena Mars, according to my unknown author, wanted the world to know hers.

There was, I noted in cross-checking these features, very little known about what Melanie Joan had done during her first years after college, other than laboring in obscurity, writing away.

When the occasional interviewer would ask about those years she would answer, "I was finding myself, as a woman and as a writer." She loved talking about how her office had been coffee shops and diners, some of which she said she worked at as a way of supporting herself, and her dream.

Her second novel sold better than the first. The third sold better than both of them. The daughter of a single parent and then no parents, the college girl who had worked her way through a small school in central New York, was richer than even she could ever possibly have imagined she would be someday.

Now here she was. As were we all, in what was showing all signs of being not just a bad week, but a full-out dumpster fire.

I closed the laptop finally and looked down at Rosie, in her usual spot at the end of the bed, my only company in this bed for quite some time, not that I preferred to dwell on that. My eyes were getting tired. My dog was already snoring softly, tongue hanging out of her mouth.

"Our landlord's story is quite inspiring," I said to her. "Maybe even more inspiring than Cassandra Demeter's, if you can believe it."

Rosie picked up her head, immediately rousing herself, as if somehow *inspiring* had at least raised the possibility of a late-night snack of some sort.

When she quickly realized there wasn't a chance of a treat, she went back to sleep. I then tried to do the same. I had no idea whether the mystery document that some-one had left for me was real or not, or if it had been written before Melanie Joan penned a similar story that would change her life. I reminded myself that in the end it wasn't my job to prosecute my client, but rather defend her. And her reputation. And keep her safe. All of the above.

But she was the one acting defensive. And probably holding things back from me, though I couldn't prove what, at least not yet. She reminded me, more than ever, of an old Kristofferson line from a song I loved called "The Pilgrim," about a man who was

119

a walking contradiction, partly truth and partly fiction.

But then maybe we all were.

I lay there in the dark, listening to Rosie's snoring, wondering about where Melanie Joan had been in those five years after college, and what her life was like when she wasn't writing her book.

If she'd found herself, I could find her, too.

I was, after all, recent events notwithstanding, a trained detective.

TWENTY-TWO

Spike called first thing in the morning, asking what he was supposed to do with Melanie Joan today. I informed him that since shooting her wasn't an option, he should stand down until he heard from me. She was in the hands of her manager for now.

"Literally," I said.

Then my father called, right before I was getting into the shower. We had entered into a deal, my father and me. He would check in with me around this time every morning, then again around midday, then in the evening. By now he had told my mother enough about Joe Doyle acting like a "nuisance" — while not entirely true, it was what he told her anyway — and convinced her to pay a visit to my sister, now remarried, almost happily, and living in Santa Barbara.

"Mom really bought the nuisance thing?" I said.

"Your mother's position was always that the less she knew about my work, the better."

"But you're no longer working."

"Irregardless," he said.

"You know what a silly word that is, right?" I said.

I heard him giggle. "I know," he said. "But sometimes I can't help myself."

"Any new developments overnight?"

"Here we go," he said. "I feel like you've practically got me on an ankle monitor."

"I'll take that as a no."

"Maybe you scared off Mr. Doyle," he said.

"I'm good, Dad," I said. "But I'm not that good."

"Or bad," he said, "as the case may be."

I didn't want him living alone while this beef with Doyle was going on. He just didn't need to know that yet, or my plan to have him watched without telling him I was having him watched. He wasn't my client, but I knew I had to treat him like one, as a way of keeping him safe. I was trying to do the same with Melanie Joan. But she wasn't making it easy, now that her current sweetie was in town. Richard Gross Points. One thing had not changed with her over the time since she had first come into my life.

She sure could pick 'em.

But she *was* still my client, at least for the time being. So I was still working her case this morning. Which is why, once I was somehow looking both as glam and as casual as I could in a Frank & Eileen denim shirt for which I'd paid far too much and white jeans that might have been a little too tight, I was in Downtown Crossing in the offices of Reddy Forensics.

I had been referred to Liam Reddy by Martin Quirk, once my father's commander in Homicide and the man Phil Randall still referred to as the greatest cop in the history of the Boston PD. Quirk, not Liam Reddy.

Reddy, who'd worked in forensic science when he himself was still with the cops, had put in his papers, started his own company, finally begun to make some real money, even though he was around my father's age.

Chapter One of the book I had started to think of as *Something* was now on Liam Reddy's desk. He had come back with the pages after being away for about thirty minutes, having taken them to the small lab at the other end of the hall. He carefully spread the four top pages out in front of him now, looking more like an ex–Marine drill sergeant than he did a cop. Stocky, steel-gray crew cut, stubby fingers, precise mannerisms. With his sleeves rolled up I saw huge forearms, and what appeared to be some kind of Army seal tattooed on his right one.

"We can date ink by testing it with a solvent we use," he said. "But again, a professional could find a way to get around it. And the kind of gel ink here has been around forever. You've probably used it in pens yourself."

He grinned.

"Want to hear about the properties the solvent can detect?" he said.

"Not so much," I said.

His grin widened.

"Didn't think so."

"Was it that obvious?"

He poked the pages with his index finger.

"You run into trouble trying to date ink back further than even a year," he said, "unless it's a specific brand that we find out was discontinued longer ago than that. And again, this ink isn't that kind of ink. So all I'd be providing to you is guesswork. And I *hate* guesswork."

"Being a science guy."

"Card-carrying," he said.

He shrugged.

"Listen, there's stuff that's possible with certain documents, involving indentations and latent imaging," Reddy said. "But I don't see any indentation worth a shit on these pages." He shrugged. "I wish I could be of more help. I mean, you are Phil Randall's kid."

"So this *could* have been written in the early nineties," I said.

"Or written last month by somebody wanting to date it and knowing what they were doing."

"Narrows it right down," I said.

"Unfortunately, science still has its limitations, damn it all to hell," he said. "But from just the preliminary testing we did, my educated opinion is that it wasn't written last month. The fading of the paper, and the ink, makes me think there's a good chance it could have come out of the time period you're talking about. But I can't say for sure. Again: Science can be like statistics sometimes. You torture it long enough, you can make it tell you anything you want it to."

He stacked the papers again, neatly, like he was making a bed with hospital corners.

"Are these pages important to your case?" he said.

"If they're real they are," I said. "Unless somebody just wants me to think they're real."

"Again," he said, "I wish I could do more for you."

"Thank you for trying."

"How *is* your dad, by the way?"

"As unchanging," I said, "as the statue of John Harvard."

"Give him my best," he said.

There was no point in telling Liam Reddy, ex-cop, about Joe Doyle, even if he was my father's friend.

"Before I go," I said, "is there any other avenue I might explore?"

"As a matter of fact, there is," he said. "The United States Secret Service."

"Seriously?"

He nodded.

"They've got a forensic database worlds beyond anything I got myself here," he said. "But they keep it under lock and key, as you might imagine. Unless it's a matter of national security, which it doesn't sound like this is."

Now I grinned.

"Well," I said, "not yet, anyway."

"Can I give you some advice?" he said.

"Oh, by all means," I said.

"Understand I'm just looking at this as a guy who spent as much time as I did with the cops," he said. "But maybe the best thing to do is forget about trying to find out when it was written and just focus on who wrote it. It seems to me that's probably the best way to get you to where you want to go."

I told him that the thought had occurred. Then thanked him again, promised I would send along his regards to my father, gathered up the pages, slipped them back inside a hard folder, put the folder into my bag, and drove back to River Street Place to walk Rosie before I headed for the office.

I had just finished locking up when Lee Farrell called me from police headquarters to tell me that my father had been arrested.

TWENTY-THREE

Lee Farrell and Phil Randall were standing in front of BPD headquarters at Schroeder Plaza, the imposing building I still thought of as new but really wasn't by now, when I pulled up. I parked at a hydrant. What were they going to do, arrest the whole family?

Lee skipped the preliminaries.

"He broke Joe Doyle's nose and Doyle had him arrested for misdemeanor battery," Lee said.

"I can tell it myself," my father said.

"So tell it."

"Farrell here already did," Phil Randall said. "He was asking for it and I gave it to him and then he had me arrested. *Me.*"

"Why don't we all walk this off?" Lee said.

Lee was well turned out, as always. Lightweight gray summer suit with faint pinstripes, white shirt, no tie. He had lost some weight lately, but no muscle, at least not as far as I could tell. Before Spike had started seeing the morning TV dude, I had tried once more, in vain, to fix him up with Lee.

"Amazing," Lee had said at the time, "that not all attractive single gay guys are automatically attracted to each other, practically on sight. What are the odds?"

Now my father said, "I don't need to walk anything off. I'm fine. When I wasn't fine is when the bastard got a rise out of me."

We were walking away from headquarters.

"Got a rise out of you in what way, if you don't mind me asking," I said.

"He called me a dirty cop," my father said. "When I was a kid, it would have been like calling me some kind of . . ."

He managed to stop himself, smiling sheepishly at Lee Farrell as he did.

"Oh, God," Lee said, "you don't mean calling you some kind of . . . *queer,* do you, Phil?"

"I didn't say that."

"Didn't have to," Lee said, grinning.

According to my father, he'd just finished an early lunch with one of his old partners, Tommy Odorizzi, at one of their favorite lunch places, Max and Leo's in Newton. When he walked around the corner to where he'd parked the car he was renting while his sporty Jetta was being repaired, Doyle was standing there, leaning against the front fender.

"Was he alone?" I said.

My father said, "I could see his SUV on the other side of the street, and could make out his goons in the front seat."

My father asked Doyle what he wanted. Doyle said he wanted to talk. Dad told him they had nothing further to talk about, unless he'd come to Newton to tell him that he was ready to cut the shit. Then Doyle said that maybe he was talking to the wrong member of the family, now that the great Phil Randall was sending his bitch daughter to fight his battles.

"I let that one go," my father said. "The 'bitch' part."

"Hey," I said, "I've been called worse."

"Same," Lee said.

The conversation predictably devolved from there, according to Phil Randall, Doyle telling him, with great relish, that before long the whole city would know what a dirty cop he was, and always had been.

It was at that point, according to my father, that Doyle had shoved him.

"Anybody witness the shove?" I said.

"Yeah. The aforementioned goons."

Doyle, who had a lot of size and a lot of weight on my father, then shoved him again, harder this time, laughing as he did, asking where I was when Dad really needed me.

"Then this guy tells me he hoped I'd never have to experience the death of a child the way he had," my father said, "and I didn't have to ask him what he meant by that because his meaning was as plain as the big nose on his face."

At that point, Phil Randall said, he stepped inside Doyle and threw the first punch he could remember throwing in years.

"Just out of curiosity," I said. "How did that feel?"

"Not helpful," Lee said.

"It felt so good," my father said, "that I can't properly describe it in front of my daughter, at least not with polite language."

"So you ended up at headquarters for a playground beef?" I said. "At your age."

"He had it coming."

"Nevertheless."

"Doyle called somebody he knew, one who owed him a favor," my father said, "and before I knew it, I was in a car on my way downtown and getting perp-walked into the building. Or at least that's the way it felt to me."

"Then I got a call," Lee said, "because Doyle made sure that the video of your dad hauling off and slugging him went viral almost immediately." He started to reach inside his jacket for his phone. "Wanna see?"

"Hard pass," I said.

"The bastard wasn't as interested in having me arrested as he was having me embarrassed," my father said.

"This can't happen again," I said.

"I'm not going to turn into some kind of shut-in," my father said. "Hiding in the house is just as bad as running away."

"I've got a better idea," I said.

Lee had told me a few days before that he was about to have some minor construction done on his condominium, maybe a week's worth, and was about to take a week off and Airbnb while it was. He called it a staycation. I told him to never use that word in my presence ever again. But on my way to Schroeder Plaza, I ran my idea past him while we were on the phone.

Now I ran it past Phil Randall.

"I told Lee he could stay with you," I said to my father.

"Not happening," my father said.

"So happening," I said.

We were in a bit of a playground staredown of our own until Lee slapped my father on the back and said, "Come on, roomie, it'll be fun!"

"I don't need a babysitter," Phil Randall said, addressing both of us.

132

We had turned around and were walking by then, stopping for traffic at the corner of Ruggles and Tremont.

"Think of it more as a bonding experience," Lee said. "And a chance to expand your sensibilities. And save me some money."

"Don't worry about my sensibilities," my father said. "They're just fine."

"Then it's settled," I said.

"*What's* settled?" Phil Randall said.

Lee winked at me.

"Wait till I tell the rest of the guys in Homicide that Phil Randall and I are living together," Lee said.

"Blow it out your ass," Phil Randall said.

"Will you listen to the mouth on him," I said.

"That's usually my line, missy," my father said.

What he didn't say was no.

TWENTY-FOUR

"Do you honestly believe that both your father and Ms. Hall are in imminent danger?" Dr. Susan Silverman said.

"Define *imminent,*" I said.

She nearly smiled.

"You first," she said.

It was our weekly session in her office on Linnaean Street in Cambridge. When I was in town and not on a visit to Paradise or an extended trip to Los Angeles on the case for Tony Gault that had made me a not unsubstantial amount of money, these sessions had gone on for years. I knew that I had aged in that time, all I had to do was look in the mirror in the morning. Or at night. Or anytime. Somehow, though, Susan Silverman had not. I knew it had to happen eventually. Maybe that was one of the reasons why I was still coming. I was playing the long game with her. She had to get old sometime.

"I just feel as if I need to look out for both of them," I said to her now. "And while I know who poses a threat to my father, I don't yet know who is threatening Melanie Joan."

"And as loyal as you say you are to Melanie Joan, we are talking about a parent here," she said. "Which raises the stakes."

"Oh, baby."

She smiled, but mostly just with her dark eyes.

"The instinct to protect people, rather than be protected, has always been a rather fundamental part of your makeup," she said. "Some might say an essential part."

"Long since established," I said.

"Oh, baby," Susan Silverman said.

She was in black today. Simple black dress, and a rare display of jewelry, pearls around her neck. No rings. Long, beautiful fingers. Hair and makeup were as flawless as ever. She was some looker. And someone I thought of as being smarter than Stephen Hawking.

"I know that others can protect them," I said. "I just feel I'm better at it. But the good news is that I'm less reluctant to ask for help than I once was."

"From the men in your life," she said.

"I even reached out to my former father-in-law for help with my father."

"Part of an ancient blood feud."

"On a good day."

"How did that work out?" Susan Silverman said. "With the both of them."

"Think of it as a fluid situation."

"So," she said, "you are once again the maiden looking to be doing the saving."

"Also on a good day," I said.

"Your instincts are clearly telling you that it will be necessary, that it's just a question of when," she said.

"Our jobs are somewhat similar," I said. "I'm just the only one of us with a concealed carry permit."

"Are you sure about that?" she said.

"Wait," I said, "you can shoot, too?"

"Like Annie Oakley," she said. "But we're getting side-tracked here, as we so often do."

Another hint of a smile.

She said, "You began today by saying that your dilemma was not being able to focus fully on one situation or the other."

"I don't have the luxury, at least right now."

"But you said you have your friend Lee with your father," she said. "And you have your friend Spike if you once again need him to look out for Melanie Joan when you aren't."

136

"When she isn't being looked after by her manager," I said, and sighed.

"Do you feel she's safe with him?" she said.

"Not even a little bit," I said.

"Oh, ho," she said.

"Pretty sure you stole that from me."

"Nope," she said. "From the man of my dreams."

"The heavyweight champion of Boston private eyes," I said.

"Well, he did fight, my cutie," she said, "but never for the title."

"Sometimes I feel as if I ought to give him a call."

"I'm sure I have his card somewhere," Susan Silverman said.

I knew we were getting near the end of my session.

"Do you believe that Melanie Joan could be a plagiarist?" she said.

"Maybe not now," I said. "But yes, I do think she could have been earlier in her career."

"And how do you feel about that?"

"Conflicted," I said. "Conflicted is the coin of the realm in here, right?"

"Something else long since established."

"But at the same time I really do feel as if I owe her," I said.

"Whether she's lying to you or not?"

I nodded.

"So the conflict lies, so to speak, in the fact that if you do find out who left the knife and the book and broke into your office, you will somehow be validating the lie. Or at least enabling it."

"What I'm really wondering," I said, "is why, if she is a thief and a liar, she would hire me in the first place."

"Maybe the one who's conflicted is your client," Susan Silverman said. "And, just maybe, the greatest threat to your friend Melanie Joan is herself."

"Why I pay you the big bucks," I said.

TWENTY-FIVE

A few minutes after six, Melanie Joan came walking into what was still her house, unannounced and unapologetic for having not contacted me, nor Spike, all the live long day, even though we both just assumed she'd been with Richard Gross.

I immediately went with an old standby.

"We need to talk," I said.

You find a good line, stay with it, and hope that it will eventually produce results.

Rosie and I were in the living room watching Maria Stephanos do the news on Channel 5.

I muted her.

"Talk, talk, *talk*!" Melanie Joan said. "All you ever want to do is talk!"

"You sound like Eliza Doolittle," I said.

She ignored that one. Or it simply went right over her head.

"Can't we just have a glass of wine and then go have a nice dinner and have some fun for a change?" she said.

"Without talking?" I said.

"Cute," she said.

"Aw, shucks," I said.

"What is it we need to talk about now?" she said.

"Your past," I suggested.

"Which part?"

"The part after college."

"Melanie Joan," she said, lapsing into the third person as she occasionally did, "was *such* a dull girl in those days."

"Somehow I doubt that."

"Well," she said, "you'd be wrong. Nothing to see there, move along."

"So you say."

"Only because it's true."

From the time I had first met her, she had seen the world as she wanted it to be, not as it really was.

"Maybe if I had a better understanding of where you come from," I said, "I could get a sense of how we got to where we are."

"Oh, Sunny, don't you know by now that my life is an open book?" she said.

I fought the urge to ask if she were discussing original material, or adapted.

"We can talk at dinner," she said. "You pick the place."

I stood down, telling her I'd make us a

140

reservation, though I didn't feel much like going out. But I decided to hedge my bets just slightly, asking her if she minded if I invited my father and Lee Farrell to join us along with Spike. She asked if they were both cute. I told her that the cuteness factor, with both of them, was through the roof. Particularly with my old man.

"But before you get any ideas," I said, "my father's the most married man in America, and Lee's also gay."

"Well," she said, "nobody's perfect."

My father and Lee agreed to dinner. They met us about ninety minutes later, after what I thought was extended prep time for Melanie Joan, at a big round upstairs table at Abe & Louie's overlooking Boylston. My father was courtly, kissing Melanie Joan's hand when I introduced them. Spike lied his ass off and told Melanie Joan he missed her even though they'd been apart for just one day. Lee reminded Melanie Joan that he was an active member of the Boston Police Department, in case anybody stepped out of line.

"Finally," Melanie Joan said, "I've got cops around when I need them."

I couldn't help smiling at the sight of Phil Randall and Lee seated next to each other on the other side of the table. An Odd

Couple if there ever was one. The retired Homicide cop and the young gay one. I was already imagining the possibilities in Hollywood for a series.

After we'd all gorged on steak, we were sharing key lime pie and Abe & Louie's skillet cookie and seven-layer chocolate cake.

"What the hell," Spike said. "My feeling is that cholesterol can only kill you once."

I'd asked Melanie Joan where Richard Gross was. She said he was taking a night flight back to Los Angeles.

"I miss him already," she said.

"Who wouldn't?" I said.

She had poured the brandy she'd just ordered into her coffee and took a drink.

I said to Melanie Joan, "I've done some new reading on the life and times of the girl formerly known as Melanie Joan Krause."

"Borrrring," she said in a singsong voice.

"Not to me," I said. "I want to hear more about what it was like when you were writing your first novel."

"Ah, my salad days," she said. "And not just because we are talking about various eateries."

She drank more of her brandy-laced coffee and said, "Yum."

"Was there anybody helping you?" I said.

"Helping me *write*?" she said in a snappish tone. "Helping me come up with ideas? No, that was all me, Sunny. Somebody once wrote that writing was easy. All you had to do was open a vein and bleed."

She smiled at me, completely without warmth, and held out her wrists.

"Want to see my scars?" she said.

"I didn't mean it that way," I said. "I'm no writer myself, but I've heard that most writers have a first and trusted reader. Sometimes more than one. I was just curious about who yours might have been. Maybe your first husband?"

"He was more a mentor than a teacher," she said. She giggled. "But that was in bed."

She had the coffee cup in both hands, and stared at me over it. I didn't know why I felt as if I was about to be lied to, but somehow knew I was. I wasn't a writer. But considered myself to be a pretty great reader. Of people, mostly.

"But the person who really turned me into a writer," she said, "was my first editor, after all my years of writing and rewriting, and after he agreed to publish me." She finished the coffee and put the cup down. "He took my first draft and sent me back to work. More hard, lonely work, just with him looking over my shoulder this time. The rest, as they say, is history."

Spike decided to lighten the moment, musically.

"She did it her way," he sang, as if his fist were a microphone.

Melanie Joan insisted on paying the check. I let her. I got a glimpse of the total, before tip, when the waiter placed it in front of her, and wanted to ask the kid if we'd broken a window. Or maybe we'd been at the table so long that it was like some sort of time-share.

My father and Lee called an Uber. Melanie Joan suggested we walk off the wine and steaks and desserts. Spike and I were game for going the distance if she was. Melanie Joan said she hadn't walked this morning, feeling the need to inform me that she and Richard Gross had been otherwise occupied.

"Too much information," I said.

"But I thought gathering information was your business," she said.

"She likes to pick her spots," Spike said.

We walked up Boylston to Arlington, made the left, cut diagonally across the Public Garden to Charles, then finally to the end of River Street Place. Spike said he was calling his own Uber now and heading over to Spike's just to see if they were having any fun there without him.

I took Rosie out for her final tour of the neighborhood. Melanie Joan stayed behind to have what she called a grand finale of a nightcap.

When Rosie and I were back she said, "See, we managed to get through almost an entire evening without talking too much business."

"It's your business that's at risk," I said. "Which is why we need to talk more in the morning."

"Damn it," she said, "I was afraid of that."

It was two in the morning when Frank Belson woke me up and asked if it was true what he'd heard, and that I was working with Melanie Joan Hall again. I told him he wouldn't be calling if he didn't already know that was true.

"But just to be sporting," I said, "why do you ask, Frank?"

I was sitting up, wide awake. So was Rosie the dog.

"Because somebody just cut her manager's throat at the Myrtle Street Playground," Belson said.

TWENTY-SIX

I considered my options on how to tell Melanie Joan, and when, but finally decided that there was nothing to be gained by waiting, and went upstairs and gave her the news about Richard Gross as gently as I could. It was like awakening someone and walking them straight into a nightmare.

Gentle didn't work, as I knew it wouldn't.

"Nooooooo!" she wailed.

She got herself upright on the bed, hugging herself, making me repeat the news, crying hysterically, rocking from side to side, her hysteria only becoming worse when I then told her how Gross had died, and where, and that I was on my way over to the playground, only a few blocks away, to find out more.

I then called and woke Samantha Heller and gave her the news about Gross and asked her to get over to the house as quickly as she could. I told her to sit with Melanie

Joan while I went over to the crime scene, and to bring any good drugs she might have with her. She told me Melanie Joan's drugs were much, much better, and that I could trust her on that.

Samantha was still staying at The Newbury. I heard her at the front door about fifteen minutes after I called. By then, the only medication I'd given Melanie Joan was brandy. If she was going to medicate on top of that, Samantha and God could sort it all out.

Samantha looked a lot more put together than I felt considering the hour. As I walked out the door, I heard another long, mournful wail from upstairs.

I'd put on running shoes, knowing I could jog to the Myrtle Street Playground as quickly as I could get in the car and drive over there and try to find a place to park even at the fringes of the police activity I knew I'd encounter when I got there.

I quickly made my way up Charles to Joy to Myrtle. As I ran it occurred to me that the neighborhood wasn't so far from where Alex Drysdale, the hedge-fund guy who had tried to steal Spike's, had been shot to death. Beacon Hill, I decided, was clearly going to hell in a handbasket.

I saw all the flashing cop lights as I ap

147

proached the playground. I knew the block well, because sometimes Rosie and I would take an extended walk and I would let her run around unleashed, and frolic a bit with other dogs, preferably smallish ones. I also knew that the Myrtle Street Playground closed at 11:30.

Just not tonight, apparently.

Belson spotted me as the first uniform I encountered at the entrance tried to stop me. Frank was standing near where there had once been a turtle sculpture, until the parents in the neighborhood decided the bronze got too dangerously hot in the summer. The headlines had called it Myrtle the Killer Turtle at the time. Jesse Stone used to talk all the time about the kind of shit you managed to remember in the night.

"Let her pass," Belson said.

"Friend of yours, Lieutenant?" the uniform guy said.

"Depends on the occasion," Frank Belson said.

It had been a cool evening. Belson would have been wearing his raincoat even if it had not been. As always, he had an unlit cigar in his hand, which he carried around with him like it was a security blanket. As I made my way to him, he was making small turns and ooking around at the playground. The long

148

circular bench. The stone wall behind it. The red-brick buildings that formed the real perimeter. The playground itself, with slides and monkey bars and the rest of it. The wrought-iron fencing, and gate through which I'd just entered. There were enough squad cars, lights continuing to flash, to accelerate night getting closer to dawn. Truly the whole area was lit as if a movie were being shot here, this one about murder. Always the main event, in the movies and in real life.

I knew that in an hour or two, whenever Belson was back in his office at Schroeder Plaza, beginning to unpack everything he'd seen here, he would remember every detail of his crime scene, right down to the colors of the swing set and slides, as if he'd been snapping one picture after another with his phone.

He had, I noted, grown a beard since I'd last seen him. But then he'd always looked as if he needed a shave, day or night.

"A beard, Frank?"

"Lisa thinks it makes me look younger, even with the gray."

"Does it tickle her when the two of you make out?"

He deftly used the cigar to give me the finger, then quickly got down to business

"Whoever did it knew *how* to do it," Belson said.

I knew he was going to tell me how, in more detail than I required, nothing I could do to stop him.

"Severed the windpipe below the larynx," he said. He made a slashing motion with his index finger. "That way there was no screaming. You do it right, and it looks like this guy did, once the carotid artery gets cut, no blood can reach the brain. But it sure can make a goddamn mess."

"Glad I didn't arrive sooner," I said.

"The whole thing, end to end so to speak, takes about half a minute, if you get the right spot first try," Belson said. "Which our killer did."

He chewed on the cigar a bit, took it out. I often wondered how many he went through in a day, and when he decided to break out a new one, and why.

"How long ago do you think it happened?" I said.

"ME is only guessing for now," he said. "But she thinks it might have been around one in the morning, or thereabouts."

"Nobody saw or heard anything?" I said.

He shook his head.

"It happened over there, far end of the nch, right in front of the wall." He pointed

150

at the red-brick building over my shoulder, one higher than most in the neighborhood. "Even if somebody had heard something, there's no clear line of sight, almost from any direction. So whoever did it also knew where they wanted him sitting. Angle of the wound says it got done from behind."

"You think he knew the person who did it?" I said.

"Or came here to meet whoever did it," Belson said. "Like I said, when it happened it had to have happened fast. And quiet. Then no oxygen to the brain. Adios."

"The only thing that makes sense to me," I said, "as if there's any sense to be made here, is that Gross must have come here thinking he could find out something about who's been harassing Melanie Joan."

"Somebody's been harassing her?" Belson said.

I told him.

"So somebody thinks your dear friend, the one who writes the hot-sheets books, actually *stole* that shit?" he said.

"You can't possibly have read one," I said.

"Lisa," he said. He shook his head. "Don't judge."

"Well," I said, "Melanie Joan thinks of them as romance novels set against a world of adventure and even mystery."

"You read *that* somewhere."

"So I did."

We both were seated on the bench by now, the other end of it from where Gross had been found. A guy taking a late-night walk with his dog was the one who had called it in. He saw Gross on the bench and thought he might be a drunk, or a homeless person. Or both. The gate was open. The dog walker didn't like that. People who lived in buildings surrounding the playground, Belson had already learned, had keys. Like a club they joined. The last one out was supposed to lock up. The first one in the morning opened the gate back up. The guy was going over to roust the slumped figure on the bench when the dog went crazy.

Then the guy saw all the blood.

"Where's the knife you told me about?" Belson said. "The one stuck in the book?"

"My office," I said, telling him I'd had Lee Farrell dust it for me.

"Nice to have the BPD on twenty-four-hour call," Belson said. "Must streamline things for you considerably."

"Can I help it if people want to help me?" I said.

"I'm gonna need to see that knife," Belson said. "Maybe it's part of some freak's collection."

I knew cops were already canvassing the neighborhood. I had done the same thing when I was a rookie, fanning out along with everybody else. Pictures were still being taken of the playground. Playground as crime scene. I got up and walked to the other end of the bench and saw a sickening amount of dried blood. Richard Gross's.

He'd told me he could take care of Melanie Joan and hadn't realized that what he really needed was somebody to take care of him. Watch *his* back. Literally.

I saw Belson scribbling in one of his spiral notebooks.

"He was supposed to be flying to L.A. tonight," I said. "Gross."

Belson said, "I already checked with the Mandarin. Looking for incoming calls. He got one about seven o'clock, about the time he should have been leaving for the airport. Then another at midnight."

"You able to get the number?"

Belson snorted. "You're not gonna believe this," he said. "But both calls were placed from a bank of pay phones at the bus terminal at South Station."

"There's still pay phones?" I said. "I thought they disappeared about the same time boom boxes did."

Belson put away his notebook. "Why *does*

153

a guy come to this spot in the middle of the night?"

"He and Melanie Joan were sleeping together," I said. "Maybe he really did want to be her hero."

"Maybe he thought he was a character in one of her goddamn books," Belson said. "Poor bastard didn't know that you're the one who wants to be the hero of every drama."

"I prefer to think of it as progressive feminist advocacy," I said.

Belson squinted at me. "You talk an amazing amount of shit. You know that, right?" he said.

"Sadly," I said, "I do know."

"You think there's more going on here than someone looking to get even for Melanie Joan copying off somebody else's paper?" he said.

"My father told me one time that murder's not just about motive," I said. "It's about stakes, too. And that the sooner you identify them, the sooner you can crack the case."

"So what are the stakes here?" Belson said.

"Wish I knew," I said.

I stood up. Looked at my watch. Past three in the morning. I was hoping that Melanie Joan would be asleep when I got back to River Street Place.

154

"But I've got to level, Lieutenant," I said. "I'm starting to think that the things I don't know about this case could fill a book."

"Book reference," Belson said, nodding. "Got it."

TWENTY-SEVEN

When I arrived at the house Samantha informed me that Melanie Joan was well sedated and back to sleep at last.

"I gave her the pill I like to think of as the big boy," Samantha said.

"She must have really liked that guy," I said.

Samantha shrugged. "She likes them all," she said. "All the way back to when she married one of her former professors."

I thanked her for coming and told her she needed to go get some sleep, because she had a long day ahead of her. She smiled and said we all did. I had only just met her. But I liked her. And told her that now.

"Don't sound so surprised about liking me," she said. "Agents are people, too."

"It should be a T-shirt," I said. "Now, go get some sleep."

"Well, *that's* not going to happen," she said.

I fixed cups of coffee for both of us. I knew I wasn't going to sleep, either. We sat in the kitchen.

"You didn't have much use for Richard Gross," I said.

"And as I know you could see, the feeling was almost breathtakingly mutual," she said. "But *this*? His throat cut? My God."

She ran a hand through her hair. She still looked way better than she should have in the middle of the night.

"What in the world was Richard doing there?" she said.

"Whatever it was," I said, "he thought it was important enough for him to spend another night in Boston."

"Maybe it was ego," she said. "Maybe he wanted to show he could crack the case before you did."

I grinned at her. "As if such a thing were even remotely possible in a civilized society."

I sipped some coffee. Delicious. Dunkin'. I'd been raised to believe that there really was no substitute.

"When Gross was here," I said, "he said something about possibly having a lead on the email."

"I heard the same thing," Samantha said.

"Did you follow up?" I said.

Now she grinned. "We didn't have that

157

kind of relationship," she said, "when we had any kind of relationship at all."

"If he had found out anything," I said, "you'd think he would've mentioned it to Melanie Joan."

"Unless he thought he was about to find out something tonight," Samantha said, "and never got the chance."

We sat in silence. There was blessedly no sound from upstairs.

"May I ask you a question?" she said.

"Make it a softball."

"How can you take something like what just happened in stride?" she said.

"Do I sound callous?" I said.

"No," Samantha said, "I wasn't suggesting that. But I'm just barely holding it together and I didn't even like the guy."

"It's all a bluff," I said. "I got rocked tonight the way we all did. I saw the blood. But I don't have the luxury of going to pieces."

"I get it."

"By the way?" I said. "How are you going to work this when *you* have to get to work?"

"By making sure that no one could ever possibly think that Melanie Joan's relationship with the noted power broker Richard Gross was anything more than professional," she said. "And that his death was a random, tragic event that has shocked her the way it's shocked us all."

"Take the personal out of play."

"Way, *way* out," she said. "And then Melanie Joan goes back to work when the series actually begins principal photography. You know that in addition to everything else she's executive producer, right?"

"I thought that was a name-only thing for the credits," I said.

"Not to her," Samantha said. "She's already letting the line producer and the director know who the boss lady is. Or bossiest lady. This is the one about how if you're not the lead dog, the view is always the same."

"Or lead bitch," I said.

She grinned. "A lot of that helpless-little-girl act is just that," Samantha said. "An act. She told me one time that most people think it's derogatory when they get called a bitch. But she said she thinks of it as a badge of honor."

Samantha Heller sighed. "And as callous as *this* sounds," she said, "this is going to make her even more famous than she was already. Once word gets out about Richard, there's going to be a huge spike in her sales on Amazon, wait and see."

"Good times," I said.

"Just sayin'," she said.

"Now we just have to make sure that we keep her safe," I said.

"You think she's in even more danger now?"

"Put it this way," I said. "She's not in any less."

TWENTY-EIGHT

Chapter Two of the unknown author's manuscript was waiting for me outside my office this time.

By now Melanie Joan and Samantha were on their way to The Newbury, where Samantha had booked a function room for the press conference about Richard Gross's murder. Melanie Joan had finally come downstairs wearing a black Brunello Cucinelli dress, ready to go play the part of grieving friend, since grieving mistress, the role she really wanted, was out of the question.

I knew it was a Cucinelli because she told us all, Samantha and Spike and me, before she went back upstairs to change her shoes.

"She seems to have rallied," Spike said. "At least sartorially."

"For the best possible reason," Samantha whispered. "Cameras and microphones await."

I watched them get into Spike's Mercedes and drive off. I had decided to skip the show, already thinking about how I was going to keep her safe going forward without asking Spike to put his life permanently on hold. I knew he'd do it for me, being Spike. I would do the same for him. But I wasn't going to ask him.

I walked to the office, taking my time in Chamber of Commerce weather, temperature in the low seventies, no clouds, trying not to project about the immediate future. Mine, Melanie Joan's, even Spike's. Before she'd gotten dressed, Melanie Joan and I had spent a long time at the kitchen table, as I explained that it simply wasn't logical to believe Richard Gross's death wasn't bound to her current circumstances, and the threats against her, and the danger she was still in. That, if anything, the threat level had now been raised to whatever was highest, orange or red. I could never keep my threat colors straight.

But she seemed secure in the belief that all she needed was Spike, and me, to protect her from everything, including another insurrection.

I walked across the Public Garden to Boylston and then made the right and went up the stairs and saw the white padded

162

envelope on the floor, with my name written in Magic Marker on the outside.

I picked it up, unlocked my new and improved Schlage deadbolt, sat down behind my desk, opened the envelope, and immediately saw this written across the top page, in what I had a bad feeling was real blood this time:

Who's next?

I didn't hesitate and called Frank Belson and told him what I had. He asked where I was. I told him my office. He said he forgot I had an office, and that he was on his way. While I waited, I read the pages, with *A Girl and Not a God* open next to them. Once again it was the same story beginning to unfold. And these pages had the same handwriting, same faded yellow paper as Chapter One.

Belson arrived twenty minutes later. He bagged the top page and said he was going to take it to the state police lab himself. But then he had never been one for delegating, any more than his former boss, Martin Quirk, had. His new boss, a woman named Glass, made him seek any possible opportunity to get as far away from her, and the office, as possible.

"Are you thinking what I'm thinking?" I said to him.

"Jesus," he said. "I hope not."

"It's going to be Gross's blood, isn't it?" I said.

He was out the door without answering me. He called a few hours later from the lab in Sudbury.

"It's a match with Gross," he said.

There was a pause.

"A message written in blood?" Frank Belson said. "What the fuck?"

I told him he'd taken the words right out of my mouth.

TWENTY-NINE

"You broke up with Jesse," Vinnie Morris said.

We were having coffee in the North End, an outdoor table at Caffe Lil Italy. It was a few blocks away from Richie Burke's saloon, which was the true love of Richie's life after his son, Richard. And me, he constantly pointed out. I'd mentioned once that I was happy just to be on the medal stand.

"Why do you persist in saying the saloon is ahead of you?" Richie had said.

"I'm a realist," I'd said, "even though I prefer thinking of myself as a dreamer."

"Jesse broke up with me," I said now to Vinnie.

"Not what he says."

"Doesn't matter," I said. "He's with Rita Fiore now."

"Man needs a hobby," Vinnie said.

He was sipping an espresso, drawing the process out, as if that would make him forget there was hardly anything in his cup. I'd never gotten the espresso thing, even at places like this that bragged about being famous for their espresso. It had always tasted to me like yesterday's coffee, at least until I started adding sugar, which espresso lovers viewed as some sort of felony.

I shared all that with Vinnie.

"You ask me here to share your fascinating theories on coffee beans?" he said.

"Just making conversation," I said.

"Always a passion of mine," Vinnie said.

"I'm trying to get you to change your mind about going off on another job."

"Told you I would if I could, but I can't once I give the guy my word," Vinnie said.

I couldn't remember him looking like anything other than a sharp dresser, and even when he was saving my life one time, he still brought the word *natty* to mind. Today was no exception. Light blue, windowpane sports jacket. White linen shirt. When he leaned back and crossed his legs after smoothing out his slacks, I saw that his shoes were the color of butterscotch. His mannerisms, as always, were as precise as a neurosurgeon's. If there were best-dressed lists for guys who could still shoot the numbers off a credit card, Vinnie would be on it every year.

The lines of his jacket were so perfect I wondered where he kept his gun.

"Gimme the full story," he said. "Maybe I can give you a few suggestions about how to handle what you got going on here before I split."

"It's complicated," I said.

"What isn't with you?" he said.

It sometimes came out as "wit" you.

"You sound like my therapist," I said.

"Bet Susan's got suggestions, too," he said. "I sometimes think she could straighten out the Celtics."

He knew Susan Silverman.

"No shit," I said.

Being a trained detective, I might have detected a hint of a smile.

I told him everything that was going on. Both fronts. My father and Melanie Joan. Telling it with an organized timeline, from Melanie Joan hiring me, through Richard Gross's death, to the message that came with Chapter Two. Vinnie took it all in, completely impassive, not interrupting. He and Frank Belson were on the opposite side of most things. I knew Vinnie had indeed whacked a lot of people in his life. But he and Belson had something in common. Neither one missed very much. Or needed things repeated.

"You and Spike can handle this, with maybe one more person you can trust to fill in," Vinnie said. "You can put a lot on that guy."

He was still working on his espresso. How was that possible?

"Toughest gay guy *I* ever met," Vinnie continued.

"Pretty sure you don't need the word *gay*," I said.

Vinnie raised an eyebrow.

"He turn?" he said.

"I meant he's the toughest guy either one of us has ever met," I said.

"Present company excluded," he said. "And a couple of other guys I know."

"Well," I said, grinning. "It's nice for me to be in the conversation."

"I meant me."

"I know," I said.

"Can't you and Spike tag team on Melanie Joan like you been doing?" he said. "I mean, for as long as it takes."

"Yeah," I said. "But just not this week. I need to make a trip of my own to upstate New York, where Melanie Joan is from, and try to fill in some gaps on her younger and more vulnerable years."

"*Gatsby,*" Vinnie said. "Younger and more vulnerable."

I raised my eyes. Melanie Joan wasn't the only one who could quote *Gatsby.*

He shrugged again. "There's a lot of layers to me."

"Let me know if you finish your thing in Texas early," I said. "I'll probably still need you the way *my* thing is going. And so you know? Melanie Joan would be the one paying."

"Wouldn't be doing it for her," he said. "No matter how much she paid me. Be doing it for you."

He flicked something off the lapel of his jacket.

"You want my opinion on this shit before I go?" he said.

We both knew it was a rhetorical question.

"This broad must have done it to make somebody come after her this hard," he said.

"There's easier ways to kill people than cutting their throat," I said.

Vinnie made a gun with his right hand. "Bang," he said. "You're dead."

"Somebody wants to scare her to death," I said.

"Maybe before they go for the real thing," he said.

"Something out of her past," I said, "and somebody."

169

"Who says she took something didn't belong to her."

"But there's still been no money demand," I said.

"Maybe there ain't gonna be one," Vinnie said. "Maybe this never had nothing to do with money."

He called for the check. I told him it was on me. He just slowly shook his head and signed the check when it came. I looked across the table. His penmanship was as neat as a Catholic school student's.

"Whoever this person is, it's some sort of wingnut," he said. "So you need to keep in mind that if he came for Gross as a way of getting to her, he can come for you, too. Like the guy did that other time I had to shoot."

Bobby Toms. Illegitimate son of Richie's Uncle Felix. And killer. Toms had thought Desmond Burke was his father, which was why he started killing people close to Desmond before Vinnie shot him.

Before Vinnie left he said, "I ain't giving up on you and Jesse."

"You silly old romantic," I said.

"Fuckin' right," he said.

When I was in the car on my way home, Frank Belson called. He asked if I had a theory on why Richard Gross had placed a

170

call to the prison in Concord the day he died.

THIRTY

The last time I'd seen Frank Belson before the Myrtle Street Playground was when a Russian had shot Alex Drysdale. Now I was seeing him for the third time in less than twenty-four hours, he and Melanie Joan and I sitting together in my living room.

"Gross didn't just call Melvin," Belson said to Melanie Joan. "Turns out he went to see him."

"Impossible," Melanie Joan said.

"Improbable, maybe," Belson said. "But not impossible. There's a difference."

"Richard would never do something like that," she said, still discussing him in the present tense. "And he would certainly never do something like that without telling me first."

Belson's response was somewhere between a sigh and a groan.

"I actually agree with you on the last part, Ms. Hall," he said. "But let's us, you and

172

me, stop dicking around here and you tell me why your manager might have been talking to your ex-husband."

At least Belson didn't call Gross her lover, even though I had told him that's exactly what he had been.

"I don't know!" she said.

"Did he ever mention to you that he knew John Melvin?" Belson said.

She shook her head vigorously from side to side. "This must be some sort of huge misunderstanding," she said. Now she closed her eyes, as if she could make an upsetting subject like this go away by refusing to look at it.

When she opened them she said, "Maybe he thought John had something to do with the situation with which Sunny is helping me."

"Melanie Joan," I said. "Lieutenant Belson knows about your situation."

"Well, maybe that's it!" she said, brightening. "Richard went to see John because he wanted to warn him to leave me alone. Or else!"

"Or else what?" I said. "Have him arrested?"

And there was, I decided, no point in asking her what *or else* might have involved.

Belson had explained to Melanie Joan that

all calls involving prisoners at MCI-Concord, both incoming and outgoing, were logged, and the person at the other end of the line identified. The guard on duty had told Belson that Melvin's caller had identified himself as his lawyer.

Richard Gross.

Whether he was still practicing law or not, he hadn't misidentified himself.

"I can't explain it," Melanie Joan said. "But all I know is that Richard would never have anything to do with scum like John Melvin."

They were going around in circles, but Belson didn't seem to mind. I had seen him work before. And I had seen him lose patience with people whom he was questioning. But he wasn't there yet with Melanie Joan.

"Yeah," he said now, an amused tone to his voice. "Big-time lawyers never end up with low-life clients. Where*ever* did I get an idea like that?"

"There's no need for sarcasm," Melanie Joan said.

"Why the hell not?" Belson said.

"He wouldn't do this to me!" Melanie Joan said. *"Richard loved me!"*

He seemed surprised that she'd blurted it out, not that it made much difference to

174

Frank Belson.

"For the last time," he said, "you're telling me that Gross never mentioned a business relationship with Melvin?"

"Never," she said.

"And you had no idea that he was stopping at the prison."

"No . . . no . . . *no!*" she said.

I thought she might be on the verge of tears.

"Why are you asking me these questions when you should be asking John Melvin?" she said, shouting at Belson suddenly.

Belson smiled.

"I plan to do that first thing in the morning, as a matter of fact," Belson said.

I asked if I could ride along, if I promised to be good.

"Don't make promises you can't keep," he said.

I told him I'd take that as a yes.

"Maybe you'll learn something," Belson said.

THIRTY-ONE

It didn't take long for Melvin to realize that the rules of engagement were different this time, and that acting like some aging lounge lizard wasn't going to get him anywhere with Frank Belson as part of the contact visit.

Nor would the fact that he'd cleaned himself up by shaving off his own beard.

"So nice to make your acquaintance, Lieutenant Belson," Melvin said after he'd greeted me.

"Kiss my ass," Belson said.

Melvin smiled at him.

"How about you kiss mine?" Melvin said.

Belson smiled back. Shook his head sadly. And then suddenly was out of his chair and in front of Melvin's chair and casually slapping him in the face.

"Hey!" Melvin said, a shocked look on his face. "Hey, Guard, did you see that?"

From across the room the guard turned

to us, grinning. "See what?" he said.

"He hit me," Melvin said.

The guard was built like a boxcar.

"He's an officer of the law, Doc," the guy said. "He'd never make contact with a prisoner."

"He could get in trouble for something like that," I said, as if trying to be helpful.

Melvin's otherwise pasty skin was red where Belson had just hit him with a good one. Belson had sat back down and was flipping his cigar with his thumb and forefinger.

"Now that I have your attention," he said to Melvin. "You need to know a couple things. One is that I read back on you, and hope you're still in here even after Jesus comes back. That's one." He was still smiling. "The other is that I'm not here to fuck around."

"Neither am I," Melvin said. "I'm leaving."

Belson started to get up and I watched as Melvin recoiled.

"I'll let you know when we're done here, asshole," Belson said.

After apparently reviewing his options, and having realized he was going to get no help whatsoever from the guard, Melvin stayed right where he was.

"Why did you meet with Richard Gross?"

Belson said.

Melvin tilted his head slightly, as if deciding how he wanted to answer that one.

"I was considering a change of lawyers for my latest appeal," he said finally. "I figured that if Richard Gross was good enough for my Melanie Joan, he was good enough for me."

"His specialty used to be business law," I said. "But he hasn't even done his own legal work for the past twenty years."

"I read up on him when he signed on with Melanie Joan," Melvin said. "He actually did a lot of appeals work when he was making a name for himself in L.A., before his only business became show business. I thought that perhaps I could offer him enough money to get him back in court. All he could say was no."

"Bullshit," Belson said.

I studied Melvin, almost fascinated. Even here, even knowing he might die in prison, there was something about him that made him think he was superior to Belson. And perhaps to me as well. It was as if he had settled back into character, despite having just been bitch-slapped by Frank.

"If you don't believe me, why don't you ask Mr. Gross," Melvin said to Belson now. "Oh, wait."

178

"Goddamn, Melvin," Belson said. "You really think you're slicker than shit, don't you? But what I'm wondering, from where I sit, is how you think things will go for you when Sunny and me show up at whatever parole hearing there might be down the road and tell them that you told us you couldn't wait to be back on the outside so you can stalk more women, on account of you having had all this time to think about getting away with it."

Melvin crossed his arms in front of him, almost smugly. "We both know you're bluffing."

Belson was studying his cigar as if it were some kind of clue.

"Try me," he said to Belson.

Then he said to Melvin, "Why did Gross come to see you?"

"Okay," Melvin said, "*okay.* I just got him out here, on the promise of paying him a boatload of money, just as a way to fuck with my former wife. It had nothing to do with my appeal. He told me when he got here that he was *only* here to warn me to leave Melanie Joan alone. He actually told me he knew people who knew people, and that if it was me harassing Melanie Joan, something might happen to me, even on the inside."

179

Melvin put out his hands.

"The conversation deteriorated from there," Melvin said. "You can check the log. He wasn't here for very long. The next thing I knew, the poor man was dead."

"Imagine that," Belson said.

"What I don't understand is why you think I had anything to do with Mr. Gross's unfortunate demise."

"If you sent people after Melanie Joan," I said, "you could certainly make a call and have Richard Gross killed by somebody on the outside who you're working with. Just as another way of hurting Melanie Joan. And give purpose to your pathetic, shitheel life."

Belson gave me a look to tell me to sit this one out.

"You give me far too much credit," Melvin said.

"No," Belson said, "I don't."

"I hate being mocked," Melvin said.

"Pity," I said.

"You mock me sometimes without saying a word, Sunny."

"What can I say?" I said. "It's a gift."

Melvin turned his attention to Belson now. He'd recovered from the humiliation of being slapped and not being able to do anything about it. Now he actually seemed to be enjoying himself. Like he wanted to have another go at Frank.

"I hope I haven't helped you," Melvin said to him.

"Good one," Belson said. "The other assholes in here must think you're a riot at mess hall."

"We're done," Melvin said.

"For now," Belson said.

As he was walking slowly to the door, Melvin said, "The last thing I told Mr. Gross before he left this room was for him to stay safe, it was a dangerous world out there, full of random acts of violence."

He smiled at Belson one last time.

"But who'd know that better than you, Frank?" Melvin said.

The guard held the door open for John Melvin. Before he walked through it, I called out to him.

"Just out of curiosity," I said. "Who's the lawyer who had been handling your appeals?"

Melvin turned and looked suddenly, almost inexplicably, pleased.

"I've been waiting for you to ask me that question," John Melvin said.

Now I waited, too.

"It's none other than the great Joe Doyle," Melvin said.

Then he was laughing.

"Small world, isn't it?" he said, and then was gone.

THIRTY-TWO

In better times, I could have talked all of this out with Jesse Stone.

He was as much of a cop as Frank Belson was, even as a small-town chief up in Paradise, Mass. As much of a cop as Phil Randall had been, and thought he still was. Jesse had proved it again not long ago when he'd solved the murder of the mayor of Paradise, and nearly died in a shootout because of it.

When Belson dropped me at home, I went upstairs to the room I had turned into my art studio. Melanie Joan and Spike were still out, having driven up to the North Shore, to Marblehead, where the opening scenes for the new series would eventually be shot. They said they'd be back in time for dinner, but I told Spike they were on their own, I had somewhere to be later with my father.

"Mind telling me where?" he said.

I told him.

"Could you possibly live-stream it?" Spike said.

I painted for a while, a piece I had put aside but recently returned to, passionately, working off a photograph of the harbor in Stonington, Maine. I'd taken the photograph when Jesse and I had spent a weekend at an inn there, before we'd broken up. I thought it perfect. The image, not the weekend, though the weekend wasn't half bad, either. So much color everywhere, lobster boats at rest, the lobster traps on the pier, small row houses as background, a returning mailboat around which everything else seemed to organize, even the water.

I worked for about an hour in the late-afternoon light that I loved in this room. It was my way of escaping, if only briefly, Melanie Joan and Richard Gross and Dr. John Melvin and the new information that had come in on Joe Doyle. When finished I sat down at the small antique writing table I'd placed near the window and took out my trusty legal pad, and once again tried to create some sort of order out of chaos by writing things down.

There was Melanie Joan on one side of the page, and Richard Gross, and the two chapters of the manuscript, and the knife, and the blood. On the other side of the page, there was my father, and his encounters with Joe Doyle, and my own encounter with him. Even the death of Joe Jr.

And now, smack in the middle, there was the name of Dr. John Melvin, and the line I had drawn right through him, from Richard Gross to Joe Doyle Sr.

I looked at the page and thought once again of Jesse. The man whose position on coincidence had never changed, from the first time I'd met him.

"No way," he said often, "that God would leave that much shit to chance."

Belson said he wanted to interview Doyle before I did, not because he thought that being connected to Melvin connected him to the murder of Richard Gross, but because Belson wasn't much of a believer in coincidence, either. He said he'd let me know when he found out whatever he could find out, and then if I wanted to make another run at Doyle, to have at it.

But whatever John Melvin said, I knew that one thing was not in dispute, whether he had come right out and said it or not: He wanted revenge against Melanie Joan, and probably against me. And Joe Doyle wanted revenge against my father, whom he blamed for the death of his son. In some ways, it made him as unhinged as Melvin.

And Doyle the lawyer, right before my father had popped him a good one, had intimated in a ham-handed way that something might happen to me.

Now he was connected to Melvin, if Melvin was telling the truth, knowing how easy it would be for us to find out if he was lying.

Was I giving Melvin too much credit, and was I making somebody sitting in a prison cell more dangerous than he really was?

Or was the sick bastard just still playing mind games, not just with Melanie Joan, and not just with me, but with a couple powerful lawyers like Gross and Doyle?

And was it too much of a leap, or plain crazy, that somehow Doyle and Gross could be connected to each other?

I finally put down my pen and left the pad on the table. I had already cleaned off my brushes. I realized I was still wearing an old paint-splattered *Paradise PD* sweatshirt that Jesse had once given me.

Jesse.

Him again.

I thought about calling him right now, assuring him that it was a business call, nothing more, making a joke out of it, but telling him that I really could use some help on a couple cases I was working. Cases that had just intersected, out of nowhere.

Knowing he would do it for me. Knowing that I would always be able to count on him the way I could count on Spike.

And Richie.

Whom I still loved the way I still loved Jesse.

Not that it was doing me any good at the moment, romantically speaking, with either one of them.

I tapped the phone icon on my phone and went to my contacts and there was *Jesse,* right at the top of the *J*'s where he had always been. Not under *Stone.*

Just Jesse.

Then I stuck the phone in the back pocket of my jeans and went downstairs to clean myself up for another big night out with my dad.

THIRTY-THREE

Desmond Burke's position on my father hadn't changed. He was willing to help me out, but only if my father asked.

And on Phil Randall's end, nothing had changed where Desmond was concerned.

He continued to tell me that the only thing he wanted from my former father-in-law was a full confession, for all of his sins.

And yet here the three of us were, on what both old men considered neutral ground, the Tavern at the End of the World on Cambridge Street in Charlestown. It was closer to where Desmond lived, by a lot, it was practically in the neighborhood for him, something my father had pointed out more than once on our way there. But both of them liked the place, the second floor of a two-story building, its siding baby blue.

"I still don't see why I have to come to him," Phil Randall grumbled as I was looking for a parking spot.

"Because I asked you to," I said.

"How many times do I tell you I don't need any favors from the likes of him?" he said.

"And how many times do I have to tell you that the favor is for me?" I said.

I had told both Desmond and my father about Doyle's possible connection to John Melvin, and how little I liked that connection, as irrelevant to my father's current situation as it might turn out to be. Just because I considered Melvin an unrepentant psychopath, capable of anything and everything.

"I can handle Doyle," my father said.

"No," I said. "You can't. He's dangerous as hell and you're . . ."

He pounced on my hesitation, giving me no opportunity to finish my thought.

"And I'm old," he said. "That's what you were about to say, wasn't it? I can't handle this myself because I'm old."

"No," I said. "I was about to tell you that you're good, Dad. But that Joe Doyle is a very bad man."

I found a spot behind the tavern. Desmond Burke's black Town Car, of course, was parked at the front door. I could see one of Desmond's body men behind the wheel. Another that I was sure was his, a

189

kid straight from central casting, was standing guard at the door. He had a ruddy Irish face and even wore the kind of old-fashioned scally cap I'd seen pictures of Desmond wearing when he was a young up-and-comer in the Irish Mob, long before he was all the Irish Mob there was left in Boston.

Desmond was at a corner table on the other side of the bar, his back to the wall. Despite the warm weather we'd been having and were having tonight, he again wore a heavy sweater with a shawl collar. He did not rise to greet us.

"Sunny," he said.

"Desmond."

"Yourself," Desmond said to my father.

"Burke," my father said back to him.

My father and I sat down. Desmond held up a finger and the bartender came over to the table.

"Midleton neat for me," Desmond Burke said.

My father and I ordered Samuel Adams Summer Ale. I wasn't drinking scotch on an empty stomach, and with more driving to do after we left here.

No one spoke until the drinks arrived. There were no Irish toasts tonight. The two old men stared at each other, even as they drank.

"So," Desmond Burke said.

"Before anybody says another word," my father said, "I want it understood that I'm only here because of my daughter."

"Makes two of us," Desmond said. "Because *I'm* only here because of your daughter."

He took his eyes off Phil Randall only long enough to throw a quick nod at me. I nodded back.

"Good that we cleared that up," I said. "You're both here because of me. I'm flattered, truly. But we're also here because of Mr. Joe Doyle *him*self, a man neither one of you has ever had any use for."

"The difference, though," Desmond said, "is that the *maroon* poses no threat to me."

He picked up his glass and held it up to what light was coming through the window, and even smiled, before taking another sip.

"Let's get to it," Desmond said.

He shifted slightly as a way of focusing all of his old-boss self on my father.

"Ask me what you came here to ask me," he said.

"No," my father said.

"Dad," I said. "You promised me you'd hear Desmond out."

"I changed my mind," he said.

"Not the first time a copper ever took a deal off the table," Desmond Burke said.

"I already told you," my father said to me. "I'm not asking a favor from the likes of him. I'm not even going to let him pay for my drink."

"You'll ask for a favor tonight if you want my help keeping the likes of *you* safe," Desmond said.

My father slammed his mug down hard on the table.

"I'm leaving," he said.

He stood. So did Desmond Burke.

"Both of you sit back down and cut the shit," I heard from behind me.

I didn't need to turn to know that the voice belonged to Richie Burke.

THIRTY-FOUR

"You've got no call to be here, son," Desmond Burke said to his son.

"You're right," Richie said. "I don't. But that's never stopped me when I thought Sunny needed backup."

Desmond turned to look at me. Sometimes I felt I could see his eyes change to the color of water.

"Did you tell him to come?" he said.

"I told him we'd be here, and why we'd be here," I said. "But you must know by now how little success I've ever had telling your son what to do."

Richie took the empty seat at the round table between his father and me. Now he grinned at my father.

"We having any fun yet, Phil?" he said.

"I'm the one who shouldn't be here," Phil Randall said to him.

"And I shouldn't have agreed to let you come," Desmond said.

193

"That'll be the day," my father said, "when you *let* me do anything."

"I feel like I'm in a scene from *Grumpy Old Men,*" Richie said to me.

"Except Jack Lemmon and Walter Matthau were funny," I said.

"There's that," Richie said.

He wore a white oxford button-down, faded jeans. I knew without looking he was wearing penny loafers. The preppiest-looking son of a mobster I'd ever known about. There was gray in his hair now, but somehow he still never seemed to age, never looked a day older — at least not to me — than the day I'd met him, and practically fell in love with him on the spot. Even though mine was a cop family and his most certainly was not.

"This may be slightly off point," Richie said. "But you look beautiful."

"Focus," I said.

"You make it difficult when you look like this," he said.

"You can do it," I said.

He got the bartender's attention, pointed to the beers in front of my father and me, called over, and said he'd have what we were having.

"I love both you guys," Richie said after the bartender had placed his beer in front

194

of him. "But just off what I heard, you do both sound like a couple of stubborn old fools." He drank. "All due respect," he added.

He turned back to me.

"Has it been like this from the start?" he asked.

"Oh, my, yes," I said.

"Sunny explained her current situation to me," Richie said. "And that she can't watch everybody at once, and be secure that both her father and Melanie Joan are safe. Dad, she's got Melanie Joan covered with Spike and herself. But she feels that Doyle is a continuing threat to Phil here, a threat that she feels may have been elevated because of Doyle's possible relationship with John Melvin, who once tried to do great harm to my wife."

"Ex-wife," I said.

"A technicality," Richie said.

"You wish," I said.

He turned and was once again addressing his father and mine.

"So," Richie said, sounding just like his father. "Here's what we're going to do. What the two of you are going to do. For Sunny, and for me." He took another sip of his beer. "Dad, you're going to put a couple of your men on Phil, at least until Sunny gets back from the road trip she's about to take, and maybe beyond. And Phil? You're going to thank my father for agreeing to do something as generous as that. And if it turns out Spike and Sunny might need reinforcements, you'll generously provide those as well."

No one spoke. If it bothered Desmond that Richie had taken over this way, like he'd taken the room, he didn't show it. Everyone drank. It still felt like I was attending some sort of weird mixer from hell. But my father and his father were still here.

I knew there were other measures that I could have taken so as not to worry about my father while I was away, and they weren't as extreme as him taking protection from an old enemy. I knew I was probably being overly cautious. But any variables or possible slipups that I might encounter with other people I could ask to watch my father didn't exist with Desmond Burke. He was a sure thing the way Spike was. Or Chief Stone. Or Deputy Chief Molly Crane.

Or Vinnie, when he didn't have a thing in Texas.

They all did what they said they were going to do.

"I'm waiting," Richie said.

"It's not your decision to make!" Desmond

snapped, his words clipped and fierce at the same time.

"Right again, Dad," Richie said. "It's not. But if you won't do this for Sunny — and it *is* for Sunny — then I will."

He smiled then, perhaps to soften sounding as much like his father as ever.

"It's just that you can do it better," Richie said to his father.

Desmond took a long time to answer.

Finally he said, "It will be done, then, even if I'm not very happy about it." He nodded at my father. "When he asks."

My father took in a lot of air, let it out.

"I'm asking," he said. "But I'm not happy about it. I feel as if I'm aiding and abetting here."

"Phil," Richie said. "Maybe think about using the filter here your daughter so rarely uses."

"Hey," I said.

I saw my father's face redden. Then he said, "Okay."

"Isn't there something else you want to say?" I said to Phil Randall.

He turned to glare at me. But I smiled and nodded at Desmond.

"Thank you," my father said to Desmond Burke.

My father's face reddened more, at what

was clearly the effort it took for him to say those two words.

"Now, how about the two of you shake hands to seal the deal," Richie said.

"Don't overplay *your* hand," Desmond said.

He left first. When the rest of us were outside, my father asked for the keys and said he'd bring the car around. When he was gone, I said to Richie, "Thank *you.*"

He leaned in toward me, our faces very close all of a sudden, and said, "I can think of a way you can show your appreciation."

"We've talked about this," I said. "Less thinking down there. More with your brain."

THIRTY-FIVE

Spike offered to make the road trip with me to upstate New York, saying he bet Molly Crane could watch Melanie Joan for a couple days. I told him that as much as we both loved Molly, and knew she'd do it if asked, that he needed to stay behind and watch Rosie and Melanie Joan, in that order.

"Oh, poo," he said.

" 'Poo'?"

"I told you I was spending too much time with her," Spike said. "Hence my generous offer to travel with you to the heartland."

"Central New York is hardly the heartland," I said.

"To me it is," Spike said.

My father offered to go with me as well. I told him I didn't require a partner for this one, as great a partner as he had once been with the cops. Richie also offered to go with me, telling me it would be like the good old days, the two of us being a team again.

"You know what the kids say?" I said. "The good old days are now."

"What kids?" he said.

I told him I'd call if I needed him. Richie said I always said that, but rarely called.

"I did in the good old days," I said.

As I got closer to leaving, Melanie Joan became more adamant that I would be wasting my time, she couldn't see the point of poking around in what she said would have been a misspent youth, except she wasn't spending much of anything at that point in her life. But I kept pointing out that she actually seemed to have done pretty well for herself, considering that she'd written the best seller that would change everything for her.

"All work and no play, and I mean *no* play, made Mellie — Good Lord, that's what they called me in those days — a very dull girl," she said.

"Perhaps you made an enemy you didn't know about," I said. "Someone you might have thought was a friend."

"I didn't have time for friends," she said. "I was too busy working."

"You did have time to marry one of your former professors," I said.

She waved her hand dismissively.

"I should have just bought a night-light,"

200

she said. "It would have been much cheaper."

I was packed by now, my overnight canvas bag near the front door, reservation made at the Hampton Inn on Genesee Street in Utica, where, among other things, they advertised a fresh duvet every day.

"No one voluntarily makes a trip there," Melanie Joan said. "I've frequently told people that if I ever went back it would be because I took the wrong plane."

"When I was in college," I said, "I briefly dated a boy from Syracuse. I kind of liked the area."

"I liked putting it in my rearview mirror."

"Is there anybody from that period with whom you have stayed in touch?" I said.

"Not hardly."

"Not even your first husband?"

"*Especially* my first husband," she said.

"You must have some good memories," I said.

"If you find one," she said, "let me know, by all means."

I headed down to Mass Ave. and got on the Mass Pike there, heading west. Waze said the trip would take four hours without any unexpected delays. Fine with me. The last time I had put any real miles on my car was with Jesse, a weekend trip up to Bar

Harbor, a little more than a year ago, in a much better time for both of us. And a much better space, not just in Bar Harbor, Maine.

Now he said he needed a different kind of space. So did I. Dr. Susan Silverman said that people always talked about finding their truth, but that the reality was that most of the time it found you. Being apart from Jesse was my truth with him now. His truth was the same with me.

I wasn't sure how Rita Fiore, the red-headed she-wolf, fit into that ideal. Richie Burke, in his endless quest to make me both understand and appreciate hockey, had explained once when he'd taken me to a Bruins game that the key to good offense was simply filling open spaces.

Well, I thought, *Ms. Rita Fiore had sure done that with Jesse Stone.* The last time I had spoken to Jesse I had informed him that she wasn't his type.

"You're right," he said.

"I am?"

"You're my type," he said. "But how's that working out for us?"

Before that particular conversation had ended he'd said, "Who's your type, Richie or me? And you can only pick one."

"You don't get to make the rules," I'd said.

202

"No shit," Jesse had said.

I drove and tried not to think about the men in my life and listened to loud music instead. When I was with Rosie at night, alone with a book or a case or a glass of Irish whiskey, I loved listening to jazz. Today I started with the Stones, in honor of the great Charlie Watts, who'd just passed, the coolest and most laid-back drummer in rock-and-roll history. Maybe I should call Jesse and tell him that after much consideration, I'd decided that neither he nor Richie was my type, but that Charlie Watts likely had been.

He'd always seemed to know who he was. The guy who some thought was the true rock of the Rolling Stones, someone who sat back there and set the beat, whatever the beat needed to be, neatly dressed, barely changing expression. Self-contained. Clearly knowing who he was.

Like Jesse and Richie.

"Would you be more attracted to either one of them if they shared more of themselves with you?" Susan Silverman had asked me once, in her own self-contained way.

"Yes!" I said.

"No," she said quietly.

"Agree to disagree," I said.

"Has it ever occurred to you," she said in her office that day, "that the one holding back too much in these relationships is you?"

I'd smiled at her.

"Here we go with the dime-store psychology," I said.

"Hardly the going rate in Cambridge," she'd said.

I crossed into New York State. By now I was listening to Keith Urban, that cutie. I was particular about what country music I listened to, but I liked him. If I could get him away from Nicole, he could hold back as much of himself as he wanted.

Was Melanie Joan frightened of what I might find out if I started poking around at Whitesboro College? Or was she simply frightened right now, period, because of what was happening to her and what had just happened to Richard Gross?

Maybe a little of both.

If she had indeed stolen somebody else's work, then why had she hired me in the first place? I kept coming back to that.

I called Frank Belson on his office number and asked about Gross's murder and if there were any new developments.

"No," he snapped.

"Sorry," I said.

"No," Belson said. "I'm sorry. I meant to say fuck no."

And hung up on me.

I stopped about a half-hour into New York. These turnpike rest areas all looked the same to me, the way shopping malls did. I used the ladies' room and bought a Coke Zero and a guilty-pleasure Reese's Peanut Butter Cup, knowing that some might say that the combination of candy and a diet soft drink was counterintuitive. I thought of it as establishing a crucial and delicate balance to my personal nutrition.

I didn't even check Waze now to pinpoint my estimated time of arrival. I'd get to Utica when I got there. I was, I decided, having a very nice day. There were no calls from my father. None from Spike, or Melanie Joan.

It actually might have been fun to have Richie along, now that I thought about it. The last time the two of us had taken a long car ride together was when we had decided to skip the car ferry from New London to Orient Point as a way of getting out to eastern Long Island and driven all the way out to Montauk, even spending one night at the Memory Motel, but just one, in honor of the Stones.

We were together then. Just not *together* together. Before we were apart again.

On the ride back to Boston he'd said, "Why isn't loving each other the way we do, and the way we always will, not enough?"

It wasn't just late at night that you thought about things. Sometimes on I-90, heading west.

I told him if I ever figured that one out, he'd be the first to know.

I was listening to Gaga when I finally got off at exit 31 in Utica, then let Waze help me make my way to North Genesee Street, and my Hampton Inn.

I checked in, dropped my bag in a surprisingly spacious room. It was still only the middle of the afternoon, which gave me plenty of time to drive over to Whitesboro College, located on the Utica/Whitesboro line.

No music now.

Just Sunny Randall, ace detective, thinking out loud.

"Mellie Krause," I said. "Where you at, girl?"

THIRTY-SIX

I was hopeful that the woman at the Whitesboro College alumni office might be only slightly younger than Martha Washington, just because I wanted her to have been around when Melanie Joan Krause was a student.

But Jeannie Holton looked to be about my age, with short brown hair and big black glasses that she made work. And I was about to find out, quickly, that she had a sense of humor. With strangers it always made me feel as if we were somehow speaking a common language.

I started by telling her that no matter how many search engines I used, I couldn't find the year that Melanie Joan Krause had graduated from Whitesboro.

"Shocking," she said. "And here I'd always thought that Wikipedia knew everything."

She made us two cups of chamomile tea. As she did, she explained all the health benefits of chamomile. I told her that I'd heard about some of them. But, she asked, did I know that it could help with menstrual cramps.

"Don't toy with me," I said.

She blew on her tea and sipped some. I did the same. It tasted like honey. Maybe a hint of apple.

"I have been fascinated by the life and times of our school's most famous alum since I took this job," she said. "One of the reasons I came here is because I knew she had. I was hopeful there might be something in the air."

"There wasn't?" I said.

"Just from the water pollution plant over on Leland Avenue," she said.

"So do *you* happen to know what year she graduated?" I said.

"Well, now," she said. "That's the thing. She *didn't* graduate."

"You already looked it up?"

"I never had until you called. I don't recall it ever coming up before. She just told people she was a Whitesboro grad and we were damned happy to have her."

"Oh, ho," I said.

" 'Oh, ho'?" she said.

"Just something I often say when I stumble into something resembling a clue."

"And this might be one?"

I grinned.

"No clue," I said.

Whitesboro, she said, had been a small community college when it had opened in the 1970s, just a few buildings around which the current campus grew to its present size. She said that because it was such a small operation when Melanie Joan Krause had first arrived on campus, her academic records were sketchy, at best.

"Like bringing new meaning to an incomplete grade," I said.

"Like that," Jeannie Holton said.

She held up the manila folder on the desk in front of her, one that she said contained Melanie Joan's academic records. The folder looked light enough that if she let go of it, it might simply float away.

"I've noticed that Melanie Joan has said that most of her college experience had simply disappeared into the fog of time," Jeannie said. "But I think one of the reasons is that she was barely doing enough work to stay in school. Our girl is a bit of a fabulist."

I slapped my forehead.

"How could I have possibly missed that?" I said.

She poked a finger on the folder.

"And after her second semester junior

year," she said, "it turns out there's no academic record at all."

"She skipped senior year?"

"Not exactly."

"As I recall," I said, "nobody who knew me at Boston University got the impression I was chasing a Rhodes Scholarship *my* senior year."

"But did you have enough credits to graduate?"

"I did," I said. "But I was sweating out my Spanish final until the morning I got to take the walk with my classmates."

"Well, you did a lot more than Melanie Joan did," Jeannie Holton said. "She took one class her senior year, and that was a writing seminar for which no grades were even given out."

"Let me guess," I said. "It was with Dr. Charles Hall."

"Obviously you know who he is."

"The husband behind door number one," I said. "But not for all that long."

"I've done my own investigating, as best I can," she said. "She married him a few months after a graduation exercise that did not include her. By then she was working part-time at the local newspaper." She grinned again. "Or so she says."

"Wait," I said. "You think she was even

fabulizing about that?"

"I never checked," she said. "Have you?"

"Going to," I said. "Soon as I leave here."

Then I said: "I haven't been able to find a death notice, so I'm assuming Dr. Charles Hall is still among the living."

"Define *living*," Jeannie Holton said.

THIRTY-SEVEN

The *Observer-Dispatch* was located at Oriskany Plaza. The staff was back at the office, I was told at the receptionist's desk, after spending almost two years working remotely. When I told her who I was and what I was in Whitesboro working on, she said she'd be right back, and walked through their city room. Came back a few minutes later with the boss.

The name of the paper's editor and lead columnist was Tom Gorman. He didn't look like the actor Daniel Craig. But he reminded me of him, just without the James Bond accent. Not much more than my height. But definitely checking all the cute boxes.

Down, girl.

Working here.

We were in his office. He had called in an intern and told the young woman she needed to take a trip back in time for a former employee. "How far back, Mr. Gorman?" the kid had asked. "When dinosaurs roamed the earth," he said. "The Reagan administration."

While we waited for her to come back he said, "We don't give this kind of service to just anybody. But you have an honest face."

"So does Lester Holt," I said.

He laughed and did some bragging on the paper, saying it was still doing the kind of local journalism that was dying in far too many places around the country. I asked him how he'd ended up here. He said he'd ended up majoring in journalism. Said it was his idea of the American dream, after growing up a foster kid.

"Good for you," I said.

"You know what they say," he said. "School of hard knocks."

"I'd be generally more impressed with you," I said, "if not for the honest-face comment."

"I meant it as a compliment," he said.

"Telling me I reminded you of Emma Stone would have been a compliment," I said.

He laughed again. It was a good laugh, both genuine and unforced. Definitely cute.

"Have you ever read Melanie Joan?" I said.

"I plan to," he said. "Right after I finish rereading *Ulysses.*"

213

"You haven't read *Ulysses*," I said. "No one has."

"But I've read about her," Gorman said. "And I've seen the same stuff you have about her having worked here. But I frankly never cared enough to check if she actually did."

"What kind of local journalism is that?" I said.

The intern came back with a printout and handed it to Gorman. He glanced at it, grinned at me.

"She was here for what would have been one semester," he said. "September through Christmas."

"She tells interviewers she worked her way through school," I said.

"Then she must have won the lottery while she did," Gorman said. "Because according to our records, it looks like she went off for Christmas vacation and never came back. At least not back here."

"Makes for a nice story, though," I said.

"Doesn't it, though," he said. "Apparently she doesn't just make shit up in her books."

I thanked him for his time. He asked how long I planned to be in town. I told him I'd probably be leaving tomorrow. He said that left time for us to have dinner.

I was at the door by then.

"Come to think of it," he said, "you do remind me of Emma Stone."

"Too late," I said.

THIRTY-EIGHT

Before I'd left Whitesboro College Jeannie Holton had told me that she was well aware that the second Mr. Melanie Joan, as she called John Melvin, was currently a guest of the state at MCI-Concord.

Then told me that Charles Hall was in a different kind of prison. Home confinement, she said, just not for any reason having to do with the law.

According to her records, Hall was seventy-nine now, but had retired from teaching twenty years earlier, before even reaching the age of sixty. He had told the school administration that it was time for him to do some writing of his own, in the small cottage on Sauquoit Creek that he had inherited from his parents. His parents, Jeannie Holton said, had both worked until their retirement at Oneida Limited, a few miles away in Sherrill, a company famous in the area for its cutlery and tableware.

"Is his impairment physical or mental?" I said.

"Dementia," she said. "Early onset happened a long time ago, as far as anybody knows here. I'm guessing that's why he stopped teaching when he did."

She had given me Hall's address. When I arrived at the cottage I thought it might be made of gingerbread. The lawn was neatly manicured and clearly well kept. There was a white picket fence where the lawn ended, small rose gardens flanking the front door where the red-brick walk ended.

Welcome to Mr. Chips's house.

I had called ahead and spoken to the woman who answered the phone, explaining why I was in town. She had identified herself as Holly, and said I was welcome to stop by, but would be wasting my time.

"The Charles who taught us is gone," she said.

I told her that I was aware of his circumstances, but that I had come this far, and that perhaps her memories might be helpful even if Charles Hall's were gone.

"I don't see how," she said.

"Then I won't take up much of your time," I said.

"You are not easily dissuaded, Ms. Randall," she said.

"I'm thinking of putting that on my business cards," I said.

Holly answered the door. She was nearly six feet tall, wearing jeans and a man's white shirt. Being a sneaker nerd, I saw that she was rocking a pair of On running shoes. She had allowed her short hair to go completely gray. Somehow it didn't age a quite pretty face and I wondered why more women her age didn't do that. I wondered what I'd do someday when I lost the battle against gray hair. I had her at about Melanie Joan's age. Maybe a couple years either way.

She put out her hand. I shook it. Firm, look-you-in-the-eyes handshake, right out of the handshakers' manual.

"Ms. Randall," she said.

"I didn't catch your last name on the phone," I said.

"Hall," she said as she showed me in.

"Oh," I said. "I didn't know that you married him, too."

"And Charles so hated clichés in writing," she said. She grinned, almost sheepishly. "I thought I was Charles's heart's desire. I was at the college first, but he threw me over for her, maybe because she was a better writer than I was." She shrugged. "But I played the long game. I never thought they'd last, and they didn't. I was still living in Whitesboro. Lo and behold, there I was to pick up the pieces."

"How long after you were a student?" I said.

She smiled, as if her own circumstances amused her.

"Just long enough," she said. "And one thing hadn't changed. He was still far too much older than I was." She paused and then added, "Now it seems as if he was a hundred years older."

The front room was surprisingly big and sunny, and the windows open. I looked past her, toward the open doors leading to the backyard.

"He's on the back patio," she said. "I never let him out of my sight for very long, because he *will* wander off. The creek feeds into the Mohawk River. Fortunately he's never made it all the way down there."

The kitchen was to our left. When we sat down on the long sofa, I could see the back of Dr. Charles Hall's head. White hair. Seated on one of the Adirondack chairs on the patio. Staring out. I could see a writing tablet on the table next to him, a pen on top of it.

"He insists on taking the tablet out there with him every day, weather permitting," she said.

"So he does communicate with you?"

"Hardly at all."

"When he does, what is it about usually?"

"Hardly anything," she said.

"Does he ever write anything?" I said.

"Not even his name," she said. "He tried to be a writer when he was a younger man. Or so he says. It didn't take. Those who can't teach write, *right*?"

"I heard that somewhere."

She said, "Sometimes he just looks at me when I address him by name and smiles and says, 'Who's Charles?' "

"But you stay with him," I said.

"Ain't love grand?" she said.

"Are you able to take care of him by yourself?" I said.

"We have two caretakers," she said. "One is me. The other is a visiting nurse who's here when I'm not."

"That must be expensive," I said.

"I do some freelance editing," she said. "But on top of that, there's more than enough of the other money for us to live on."

" 'Other money'?"

She looked at me quizzically.

"You don't know?" she said.

"Don't know what?" I said.

"I would think your client would have told you."

"I apologize for being dense," I said. "But is Melanie Joan paying your husband alimony?"

"Not alimony," she said. "Even if the checks do come monthly."

"What checks?" I said.

"The ones from the nondisclosure agreement," she said.

THIRTY-NINE

Dr. Charles Hall's second wife, the ex-student he married after marrying Melanie Joan Krause, said that the NDA that Hall had signed after *A Girl and Not a God* had become a runaway best seller had not been ridiculously lucrative. But still quite generous, and a lot more than his salary as a tenured professor at Whitesboro College. A professor who was clearly catnip to the ladies.

"Why did Melanie Joan need to buy his silence?" I said. "Silence about what?"

"He never said," Holly Hall said.

"Not even to you?" I said.

"Charles may have had a weakness, shall we say, for his attractive female students," she said. "But he had his own code of honor, even if it didn't seem to apply to those female students in the moment."

"A weakness that would get him MeToo'ed into a pillar of salt in the modern

222

world," I said, "even if he was teaching at the most liberal of any liberal arts college on the planet."

I thought she might have colored slightly as she stared out again at her husband, who as far as I could tell hadn't moved a muscle since I had arrived.

"Those of us who did succumb to his, ah, charms never complained," she said. "And it really was a different world then, at least at good old Whitesboro College."

I waited.

"He said that a gentleman didn't talk," Holly said. "And said that he had made a gentleman's agreement. He considered his silence a small price to pay as long as the checks kept coming."

She turned to stare out at the back patio.

She let some air out. "So there was a heart attack last year, from which he recovered," she said. "But the doctors say that they just feel that even his own body is beginning to collapse on itself." She offered me an extremely sad smile. "He's shutting down at an alarming rate. But then shutting down for good would be a blessing at this point. Isn't that what we're supposed to say?"

"When he was able to communicate," I said, "did he talk much about the money?"

"Only to joke about it," she said. "He

referred to it as his own academic scholarship. And said that she could certainly afford it."

"And that was it?"

"It was," she said. "Maybe he would have eventually opened up if he hadn't shut down this way. Maybe there would have come a point where he thought we didn't need the money any longer, even though we did. I simply don't know. And will likely never find out."

"This may sound indelicate," I said, "but do the checks keep coming after he's gone?"

I saw something change in her eyes, just slightly. Lights flickering.

"There may be, ah, some dispute about that eventually," she said. "Just not yet."

"But you truly never got any sense of what she wanted him to keep quiet *about*," I said.

She shook her head.

"He told me once that he had written something about her, and that it would be up to me to decide whether to share it with the world after he was gone," she said. "But he never told me in what form it was. Or where it was."

She was talking to me but looking at him.

"He never used a computer," she said. "Wouldn't have known how to hit the power button. Never owned a laptop, or a cell phone. He was a bit of Luddite that way, my Charles. Wrote longhand. Used an old Royal typewriter. There are boxes of pages downstairs in the basement. Correspondence, old students' papers. Like that. Letters to former female students, ones from before Melanie Joan and I came along, that actually made me blush. But I have found nothing he ever actually did put to paper on Melanie Joan Hall."

I said, "It's ironic, when you think about it. She's paid him for his silence all these years. And now he's gone almost completely silent anyway."

She stared past him now.

"There was this one night, maybe five years ago," she said. "Charles liked his red wine, and was working on a second bottle of cabernet, and he was talking about why he loved teaching, the magic he'd feel when he realized there was someone in the room who understood the power of telling a good story. And I thought this might be the night when he might spill. So I asked him about Melanie Joan, something I hadn't done in a long time, what kind of writer she'd really been when he met her. He smiled then. Even now, it's such a wonderful smile, I hope you get to see it when I take you outside. We were sitting right here on this couch. He motioned me to come so close that I thought he was about to kiss me. Then he said, 'Mellie wasn't even the best one.' "

"When I asked him to elaborate, something rather sweet happened," she said.

"What was that?"

"He started to cry."

I had absolutely nothing to add in the moment.

"May I just go out and say hello to him?" I said.

"Before I take you out," she said, "let me ask you a question, Ms. Randall: Why are you here, really? You've been quite vague about that, from the time we spoke on the phone."

"It's difficult for me to explain fully," I said, "and still honor my own agreement about confidentiality with my client."

"Don't give me that fucking shit," she snapped, the force of the words, and her language, surprising me. "Do you want me to sign a nondisclosure, too, Ms. Randall?"

"I didn't mean to offend you."

"Perhaps *insult* is a better word," she said.

So I told her about the threats against Melanie Joan, and the suggestion that the work on her first novel might not be her own. And about the death of Charles Gross,

226

which Holly said she'd read about.

"Well, you can see that Charles can't help you with any of that now," she said. "Nor can I."

We went through the double doors to the patio. The pen and the empty pad were still on the table. Holly Hall set up chairs like the one in which her husband was sitting, so we could face him.

It was the first time I had seen his face.

And Dr. Charles Hall, as old as he was, as absent from the world as he was, was gorgeous, even better looking than the images of him I had seen on the Internet.

I knew I was dating myself, but with his white hair and his own black-framed glasses, he looked the way Cary Grant did when he was old. That kind of gorgeous. His vacant eyes were the color of the sky.

"Charles," Holly said gently, "you have a visitor."

If he heard her, he didn't acknowledge it. So I got out of my chair and crouched in front of him, and for some reason took his hands.

"So nice to meet you, Dr. Hall," I said, smiling at him.

He looked down at his hands, and then at me.

Then something happened to his face suddenly, and his eyes, fear or shock or both.

"You came back!" he said.

"Charles?" Holly Hall said softly.

Her husband was agitated, shouting. Not lost in his own world at all. Very much in ours.

"Just like you promised you would!"

He got up then and out of his chair and started to say something else, the fear still in his eyes, his face red with effort. But the words wouldn't come. He had to put his hands on my shoulders to keep himself from falling.

He put his face close to mine. I was afraid he might try to kiss me.

"I'm so sorry," Dr. Charles Hall whispered.

I was afraid he might cry now.

He collapsed instead.

FORTY

There were still COVID protocols in place at the Utica Community Health Center, so Holly Hall met me outside. She'd been in the ambulance with her husband. I'd driven over, planning to drive home from there and not spend the night.

"He's regained consciousness," she said.

She didn't just look tired now. But much older. My mother once said that as women aged, daylight became the devil.

"Good news," I said.

"I'm not so sure," she said. "He has shut down completely now, as if he's retreated more inside himself than ever. It seems to have been triggered by seeing you, whomever he thinks you are."

"Who *did* he think I am?" I said.

I looked more closely at her as she stared past me and across the street, perhaps taking a clearer look at how the reality for her and for her husband had somehow become even bleaker over the past twenty-four hours. I was quite sure that only other caregivers truly understood. I knew I didn't, and hoped never to find out.

"Who knows," she said. "Maybe he thought you were a younger version of me, and remembered the girl I was and the book he told me that I had in me."

"Did you?" I said.

"Oh, I started it," she said. "Doesn't everybody? He helped me quite a lot, actually, with the structure and the voice of the main character. We talked about it endlessly. But no, I never became the writer Charles wanted me to be."

She smiled.

"But one he very much wanted to sleep with," she said. "Of course, it hardly made me unique."

"I'm certain this is likely an unknowable thing for you," I said. "But if he didn't think I was you, who might he have thought I was?"

She turned back to me.

"Any of them," she said.

I told her I would check back in, perhaps in a few days, to see if there had been any improvement with him. She said that was quite decent of me, but didn't expect there to be any improvement.

"In a way," she said, "maybe you did us a favor by showing up."

"I'm not sure I understand," I said, because I didn't.

"By sending him all the way off into his own world for good," she said. "And into a place where he can get the care he needs from someone other than me. So that whatever life I have left doesn't still organize itself around the living dead."

She offered me her saddest smile yet.

"Like I said about when we were first together," Holly Hall said. "I didn't do the math."

Then she said, "I'm sorry you didn't find the answers you were looking for."

"I thought he might have them," I said.

"I'm quite sure he does," she said. "Not that it will do you much good."

She said she had to get back inside. It was fine with me. There was nothing else to be said. He had been at least twenty years older when they'd started up together, roughly the same age difference there had been between him and Melanie Joan when she had fallen under his spell, as creepy as the whole idea was to me.

Dr. Charles Hall had perhaps thought I was one of his girls, one who'd maybe written the book he'd told Holly she had in her.

Who might have been the best he ever had.

As a writer, not another sexual conquest.

But which girl?

And had that girl written a book that ended up being published under Melanie Joan's name?

Or was what was going on something other than a literary revenge tour?

I was passing one of the Albany exits on the thruway, singing along with Adam Levine, when Richie called.

"You interrupted me rocking out with Maroon 5," I said.

"Where are you?" he said.

I told him.

"Before I tell you what I'm about to tell you," Richie said, "I just want you to know that he's fine."

"Who's fine?"

"Your dad."

"What happened to my dad?"

"He was shot," Richie said.

I felt the air come out of me.

"You said he's fine," I managed.

"He was shot in the upper arm," Richie said. "A through-and-through, like when I got shot that time."

I felt myself gripping the steering wheel as if it were some kind of life preserver.

"It was Joe Doyle, wasn't it?" I said.

"Actually," Richie said, "he got hit saving Doyle's life."

FORTY-ONE

My father was already acting as if the whole thing were some giant pain in the ass. Not getting himself shot. Having to talk about it. And being fussed over because of it.

At his age, he somehow still saw himself as Dirty Harry, even if he was currently being babysat by a mobster's foot soldiers.

We were in my living room. Phil Randall, Richie, Rosie, me. And Melanie Joan, who was acting so solicitous about my father I thought she was on the verge of going out to buy nurse's scrubs. She had even managed not to ask all the questions she wanted to ask about her first husband once Richie and my father had arrived.

"I've been shot before, for chrissakes," Phil Randall was saying now. "Want to see the scars?"

"No!" Richie and I said at pretty much the same moment.

Melanie Joan smiled. "I do, Phil," she said.

Jesus, I thought. Was she actually flirting with him? Maybe older guys really were still ringing her bell.

But then, why not? After having just encountered her first husband, I realized Phil Randall did fit a certain male demographic for her, or at least did at one time.

Richie had picked my father up after he'd been stitched and released at Mass General. He'd already been questioned by a couple BPD detectives by then. And by now he'd already tossed the sling they'd given him at the hospital into the backseat of Richie's car.

He'd now been run off the road and been shot in the same week. If that wasn't excitement for my old man, it sure was for his baby girl.

"Does it hurt?" Melanie Joan said.

"Only when he bitches," I said.

Richie grinned. "If that's true, he's going to need a lot more pain meds than he left the hospital with."

"Tell me again how it happened," I said.

"I told you once," my father said.

"Humor me," I said.

"When don't I?" he said.

He had called Doyle and told him they needed to end this, and that meant ending it face-to-face. If Doyle was man enough.

Doyle had agreed. I told my father that of course he'd agree, how could he not honor the timeless codes of macho bullshit?

Phil Randall had made it happen, the meeting he'd scheduled at Farlow Park in Newton Center, by giving Desmond Burke's men the slip.

" 'The slip,' Dad?" I'd said.

"I know," he'd said. "Outdated cultural reference."

"Little bit," I said. "*How* did you give them the slip?"

"Told the boys I was having chest pains," he said. "They took me to that Brigham Urgent Care in Newton. They couldn't go in with me because they've still got those COVID rules. I flashed my badge and walked out the back door."

"You faked a *heart attack*?" I said.

"It was more of an implied type thing."

He had the Uber he called drop him off near the Richardson Street lot, not much of a walk to the appointed place in the park. I knew there was a wide expanse of central lawn at Farlow because my father had taken me there a lot when I was a girl. There was even a pond and footbridge that reminded me of the Public Garden.

My father arrived fifteen minutes earlier than he'd told Joe Doyle to arrive. He didn't think Doyle would try something in a public place. But he'd always told me that cops hated surprises even more than they hated paperwork.

Once Doyle arrived, the two of them finally sat down on the bench where my father and I had once eaten picnic lunches. Doyle told my father he was wasting his time, if he knew anything about grudges.

"And like I've told you before," Phil Randall said, "I told him I was a cop, wasting time was one of our specialties. And he told me that didn't mean I got to waste his."

The two of them went around and around on that. Wasting more time. Finally Doyle told him to get to it. And my father told him that instead of Doyle holding a grudge against him, he should be asking for my father's help to find out who was really behind Joe Jr.'s murder.

Doyle asked why in the world would my father do something like that. Because, my father said, he'd spent his whole life finding out who did it.

And then Joe Doyle surprised him by saying he'd think about it. They even shook on that. Before Doyle got ready to leave, my father asked him about John Melvin, thinking he could do me a solid. Doyle told him that he'd defended a lot of snakes in his life, but that Melvin was one who gave cop-perheads and water moccasins a bad name. And that he was finally well done with Melvin, taking consolation only in how many billable hours he'd ended up with at Melvin's expense, despite having failed, and spectacularly, on his appeals.

It was then that someone dressed like some kind of ninja, all in black, mask over his face, came riding down the bike path at full speed. My father didn't see the gun until it was almost too late, but when he did see it being raised, the man in black was pointing it at Joe Doyle. Sitting there at the other end of the bench.

He'd already told me this part, but seemed to relish telling it again.

"I have just enough reaction time to throw myself across the bench and push Doyle off it," Phil Randall said. "I get hit right before I end up on top of him."

Getting to his favorite part now.

"The guy would have probably come over and finished us both off if I hadn't cleared my weapon the way I did and got off a couple shots," he said. "The only reason I didn't hit him was because it was my right arm that had been hit, so I had bad aim. And I rushed the shot."

He'd heard a woman screaming then, and

the ninja guy had taken off on what my father said was one of those fancy red racing bikes.

Phil Randall turned to Melanie Joan then and said, "I generally hit what I'm aiming at."

"Of course you were carrying," I said.

"Like I told Mr. Doyle when we were waiting for the squad car and the ambulance to show up," he said. "Once a cop, always a cop."

I turned to Richie.

"Reminds me of something my father once said about yours," I said.

"He's said a lot of things about Desmond," Richie said. "Which one?"

"Some people cannot be rehabilitated," I said.

FORTY-TWO

Melanie Joan and I went for a good long walk along the Charles the next morning, past the Longfellow Bridge and then toward the Harvard Bridge at Mass Ave, having decided that if we didn't make it all the way to the bridge, we'd stop when one of us finally got tired.

"I don't get tired," she said.

"I do," I said.

I was tired, period. Tired from my trip to upstate New York, exhausted from trying to figure out who Dr. Charles Hall thought I might be, from over there on his side of the rainbow.

I was tired of worrying about my father, and Melanie Joan. Somebody was coming for her, clearly, the way somebody had come for Joe Doyle, after he had come for my father.

I had now spent quality time, if you could call it that, with both of Melanie Joan Hall's

240

husbands. Such a joy. Somehow her second husband, Dr. John Melvin, was still connected to me, and to her, and to Joe Doyle.

Which connected Melvin to my father.

I felt as spun around as I did when I tried to figure out the financials in *Billions.*

I looked across the river to Memorial Drive, where MIT was. The view from this side of the river, as always, was pretty sweet. Just not as sweet as it was from over there. Surely somebody at MIT could figure out what the hell was going on over here, at least with me.

The reason I had waited to have the conversation that Melanie Joan and I needed to have about Charles Hall was because I was too tired to have it last night after Richie drove my pistol-packing father home.

I had my snub-nosed .38 in the side pocket of the *Boston Strong* hoodie I was wearing this morning. I didn't really need any kind of sweatshirt, with the temperature in the low seventies. But I felt as if I did need my gun.

"Why the nondisclosure?" I said.

"Won't I be violating it by disclosing *that?*" she said.

I swallowed a sigh.

"Melanie Joan," I said. "I like you. I do.

You've been more than generous to Rosie and me with the house, even though you could ask us to leave at any time. But having said that? I am not in the mood to fuck around today."

"Can't a girl make a joke?" she said.

"What joke?" I said.

"Well," she said, "someone's in a pissy mood."

" 'Pissy,' " I said, "doesn't even begin to describe my mood, frankly."

She was wearing high-rise Lululemon tights that were *extremely* tight. But she could carry it off at her age. She kept herself up. And her figure. She didn't just try to power-walk every day. I could hear her most mornings doing a Bar Method class on her laptop. She could have afforded having a trainer come to her. But she said she liked being able to simply close her screen instead of having a trainer hurt her feelings. She had pointed out one morning that all of life should be like that.

Just close the screen.

Make the bad man — or woman — go away.

"The nondisclosure," I nudged.

"You know Charles helped me with my first book," she said. "To me the money was just a gesture of gratitude. Somewhat like alimony."

"Even if he remarried?"

"Even if."

"Why couldn't you just send him a monthly or yearly or whatever stipend without an NDA?"

"It was just like my own personal insurance policy against him wanting more someday," she said, "or trying to tell people that he had done more with my book than simply help edit it before it was in the hands of a real editor."

"*Did* he do more than edit it?" I said.

"No," she said, perhaps too quickly. "The person who ultimately did the most to shape that book *was* the real editor. Chaz."

Chaz Blackburn. Her editor at McCardle & Lowell then, and now. The publishing house was still located in Boston, in the same building where it had been for the past one hundred years, at Washington and School.

Because he had been credited with discovering Melanie Joan, and because of all the success they'd had together, he was not only the chairman of the company now, he owned a very nice chunk of it.

I had met him a couple times in the past when Melanie Joan had come to town for book launches. Blackburn was in his early eighties now, I was pretty certain. But he still edited her books and, she said, gave no indication that he was considering retirement. The company had no policy about that and it wouldn't have mattered if it did, because for all intents and purposes, Melanie Joan and Chaz Blackburn *were* the company by now.

I hadn't told Melanie Joan, but I planned on calling him later today or tomorrow, just to learn more about the circumstances of her manuscript coming to him over the transom, as publishing people liked to say back in the day. And for him to compare it to my rogue manuscript.

For now I just said, "What does Chaz think about this ghost manuscript?"

"Chaz says that the only person who can write like me *is* me," she said.

Of course he does, I thought.

"And no one has ever come to him, or anybody else at McArdle and Lowell, with the suggestion that you're a plagiarist?" I said.

I was starting to flag a little. Melanie Joan seemed capable of walking all the way to one of my old classroom buildings at Boston University.

"Stop using that word!"

"How about theft of artistic content?"

"No," she said. "No, no, no. Because there never was any."

"The current Mrs. Hall says that the romantic involvement that you shared, and she shared, with Dr. Charles was hardly unique."

She smiled. "The man did have his charms."

"Did he ever mention other students whom he thought showed real writing promise?"

"The youthful me actually asked him that question once," she said. "And he said that no one he'd ever had in class approached my ability as a storyteller. He said that every writing teacher hopes that someone with a talent like mine walks into the room someday."

"Before he collapsed he clearly thought I was someone else," I said. "Any idea who that might have been?"

There was a four-person shell to our right now, gliding through the water. It looked easy. I had tried it one time. It wasn't.

"I'm sure I don't know," Melanie Joan said. "And now, according to you, he is permanently cuckoo for Cocoa Puffs."

"Beautifully put," I said.

"Oh, God, Sunny, will you lighten up?" she said. "I'm sorry he's in the shape he's in. I am. But he will be taken care of for the rest of his life."

"For that one moment with me," I said, "he was intensely present."

"What exactly are you asking me?" Melanie Joan said.

She sounded petulant again. Another of her default positions.

"I guess I am asking you," I said, "if there's something you didn't want him to disclose about you that you haven't shared with me."

She stopped. I stopped. She turned so that the Charles River was behind her.

"You make it sound as if I have some deep, dark secret," she said.

"Where would I ever get an idea like that?"

She crossed her arms.

"Maybe I need to rethink this relationship," she said.

"Is that a threat?"

"An observation."

"Maybe we both need to rethink this relationship," I said.

I thought of how cruel sunlight had been to Holly Hall. But not Melanie Joan. Even just going out for a morning walk, she had done some banging makeup job on herself.

"I hired you this time for the same reason I did the last time," she said. "To look out for me."

"You may not believe it," I said, "but that is precisely what I'm trying to do."

"Well," she said, "it certainly doesn't sound that way to me this morning. Sometimes I get the feeling that the one really stalking me is *you.*"

With that, she turned and started walking back up the Esplanade toward River Street Place. I had no choice but to follow her, even though she was walking at an even more brisk pace than before.

But I had to admit that the walking was working for her, and the Bar Method, and the Peloton she had back in Los Angeles. I hoped my ass looked as good as hers did when I was her age.

If I wasn't in such a pissy mood, I might even have mentioned that to her.

FORTY-THREE

Melanie Joan didn't fire me when we got back to the house. She showered and went through the process of remaking her face and Spike picked her up to go shopping, before she was scheduled to have a late breakfast with the showrunner for the new series at the Courtyard Tea Room, inside the Public Library. I knew what a showrunner was by now. I had briefly dated a Hollywood agent, after all.

"Shopping always seems to pick up her spirits," Spike whispered to me on his way out the door.

I whispered back that Melanie Joan appeared to need shopping the way the rest of us needed oxygen.

"And that's supposed to be a bad thing?" Spike said.

Before I walked to my office I called Tom Gorman at the Utica newspaper.

"Emma Stone!" he said.

"Sad," I said.

"I know I can make this right," he said, and then I told him how he could start trying.

He said he'd get back to me when he knew something.

"I feel like this is a do-over for us," he said.

"Stop talking," I said. "Start digging."

"Out of the hole I put myself in?"

"Reporter-type digging," I said.

A half-hour later I was happily in my office, indulging in a second cup of coffee, reviewing the notes I'd made about my conversations with Holly Hall, when Belson called.

He skipped the preliminaries, as always.

"You know a guy named Chaz Blackburn?" he said.

"He's Melanie Joan's editor," I said. "But you already know that."

"His housekeeper found him about two hours ago," Frank Belson said.

I knew there was more. He never called with good news.

"Somebody cut *his* throat," Belson said.

FORTY-FOUR

Charles (Chaz) Blackburn, gentleman editor, lived in an old Victorian — I sometimes wondered if there were young Victorians — in the Ash Street Historic District of Cambridge, between Brattle and Mount Auburn.

I called Melanie Joan when I got to the house. She said she had just arrived at the Public Library. I asked if Spike was with her. She said he was right next to her. Then I told her that Blackburn was dead, and how he'd gotten dead. She wailed in a way that I was sure startled the decent people at the library, and then began to sob.

The next voice I heard was Spike's.

"I'll meet you guys at home," I said.

"On it," he said.

Then I called Samantha Heller.

"First her lawyer, now her editor," Samantha said. "I'm the agent. Do I need to worry?"

"There's an old line a friend of mine

uses," I said. " 'I'm not paranoid, just extremely alert.' " And I told her to head over to River Street Place and I'd get there as soon as I could.

Belson was waiting for me inside the white picket fence surrounding what had been Chaz Blackburn's front yard. The crime scene people were wrapping up their crime scening. There were just two squad cars left on the street along with Belson's. His was halfway up the sidewalk. There were a few onlookers on Ash Place. But this *was* Cambridge. Residents probably thought they could get written up for gawking.

"ME figures it happened last night," Belson said.

"Security cameras?" I said. "Doorbell cam?"

"No," Belson said. "And no."

He made an impatient gesture that took in the quaint, tree-lined street. Pretty to look at, understated, classy, expensive as hell. All the things I aspired to be.

"They probably think a security camera would fit in like a wart," he said.

"Vivid imagery," I said.

"Bite me," he said.

He told me the housekeeper came twice a week, and had found the body slumped over the desk in the study that Charles had used as his home office.

"Eighty-two," Belson said. "I looked him up. Still working. Now the poor bastard goes out like this."

He opened the gate to the picket fence and leaned against his car and took a cigar out of his pocket and actually lit it.

"Don't give me any shit about this," he said. "I've got a wife for that."

"Moi?"

"I hate to state the obvious," he said once he had the cigar going, "but you appear to have a goddamn crime wave organizing around your client, one with lots and lots of blood."

"Talk about an eye for detail," I said.

"Just for the obvious," he said.

He smoked and studied the outside of the house. He was still wearing his crime scene gloves. I was close enough to his air space to experience the full force of the cigar smoke.

"I've been meaning to ask," I said, "but do expensive cigars smell better than yours?"

"You ask me, they all smell like shit," he said.

"Why do you still smoke them, then?" I said.

"Beats the shit out of me," he said.

This was part of a familiar routine between us, the small talk that was a defense
mechanism for moments like this, places
like this, crimes like this. Belson took the
cigar out of his mouth, studied it like it was
a clue, and said, "What the hell is going on
here?"

"I think somebody is trying to hurt her as
much as they possibly can, and scare her to
death, before they try to kill her to death," I
said.

"Why the editor?"

"He discovered her," I said. "And helped
her when nobody knew who she was. If he
wasn't a father figure, he was at least an
uncle type."

"You mean helped her become rich and
famous," Belson said.

"Helped her become Melanie Joan Hall,"
I said.

"Nasty way to take people out, with a
knife," Belson said.

"We had this same conversation after
somebody did Richard Gross," I said.

"Whoever it is," Belson said, "was allowed
to get close enough to both of them to do
it."

"Or snuck up behind them," I said, "like
the fog coming in on little cat's feet."

"Carl Sandburg wrote that about cat's

feet," Belson said proudly.

"You dog, Frank," I said.

I was, I told myself again, surrounded by literary people.

FORTY-FIVE

In the time since I'd spoken to Melanie Joan on the phone, she'd skipped all the other stages of grief and gone straight to acceptance.

"He always wanted to die at his desk," she said.

We had been having a lot of group sessions in the living room and were now having another. Melanie Joan. Samantha Heller. Spike, Rosie, and me. Rosie was between Samantha and me on the sofa.

"I say that with love," she added.

"Everybody knows how close the two of you were," Samantha said. "You don't have to prove it to us."

"If you add it all up," Melanie Joan said, "it was the longest and most successful relationship with any man in my life. We made a good team, Chaz and me. But in all honesty, he's done very little work on my books for a long time. The last couple books, his line notes were practically nonexistent."

"He was murdered last night," I said quietly, as if resetting the conversation for her.

"Don't you think I know that?" Melanie Joan said. "I was just trying to get you to understand my relationship with Chaz." She looked over at Spike as she pointed at me. "Isn't she the one always accusing me of holding things back?"

"I need a beer," Spike said, and walked toward the kitchen.

His way of sitting this one out.

Melanie Joan turned to Samantha now.

"I can only cry for Chaz so much," she said. "You understand that, don't you?"

"We all do, MJ," Samantha said. "Sunny included."

"Who would do such a thing?" Melanie Joan said.

"The same person who did such a thing to Richard Gross," Samantha said.

"What we need you to understand," I said to Melanie Joan, "is that someone is closing the circle around you in a quite violent way."

"The way it likely has for all of us who are close to you," Spike said, back with a bottle of Samuel Adams.

"Some closer than others," Melanie Joan

said, shooting me a withering look. Or so she seemed to think.

"Sigh," I said.

"How are you going to protect me and each other?" Melanie Joan said.

"It can be done," I said. "But I'm going to need more help."

"More than you and Spike?" Melanie Joan said, making the two of us sound like the First Army.

"Yes," I said.

"How can such a thing even be possible?" Spike said. "I mean, who's better than us?"

I told him.

"I stand corrected," Spike said.

FORTY-SIX

I already knew where the office was, at the corner of Berkeley and Boylston. If you did what I did for a living, you thought it should be given landmark status.

Dr. Susan Silverman had said she'd call ahead to tell him that I was coming.

"Is this like a referral?" I said to her.

"More like a warning," she said. "And you did say you occasionally thought about calling him."

I knocked on the door now.

"It's open," I heard from inside.

He was behind his desk, a cup of coffee near his left hand, the right-hand top drawer of his desk open, *The Globe* turned to the comics page, an open box of Dunkin' Donuts next to his coffee.

I smiled.

"Spenser," I said.

He smiled back.

"I am he," he said.

He was bigger in person, even seated, than Susan Silverman said he was. I had known for some time, even before she came clean to me, that the man of her dreams to whom she occasionally referred was the most famous private detective in town. And the best. Present company very much included.

And despite a nose that she'd told me had been broken several times when he was still a boxer, he was exactly as she had described him:

A hunk.

And a half.

Almost as much of one as the African American man stretched out on the office couch, Thomas Friedman's new book open on his chest. He wore jeans faded nearly to white, brand-new sneakers that even I knew were old Jordans, an impossibly tight black T-shirt. Overhead lights made his bald head gleam brilliantly.

"Hi, Hawk," I said. "Pleasure to meet you."

He smiled brilliantly.

"I know," he said. "I know."

"Coffee, Ms. Randall?" Spenser said.

"Sunny."

"Coffee, *Sunny*?" he said.

I told him cream, one sugar, would be fine. He got up, poured me a mug out of a

Cuisinart pot, spooned in sugar, got some half-and-half out of his refrigerator, placed the mug on a coaster in front of me.

"A coaster?" I said. "In the presence of the two toughest guys in Boston?"

Spenser grinned.

"For Dr. Silverman," he said. "Who recently gifted me with this desk, after the old one got shot up. She prefers, rather forcefully, that I not leave rings on it."

We each drank coffee. Hawk went back to reading his book.

"So how are things going in your slasher movie?" Spenser said.

"You've spoken to Belson, obviously," I said.

"I have," Spenser said. "And to Susan."

"Did she specifically tell you why I wanted to see you?" I said.

"Just that you might need some assistance," Spenser said. "In more general terms, on the right side of patient confidentiality."

I winked at Hawk. "And now here we all are."

Hawk smiled at me again and this time I felt as if my heart might have just possibly skipped a beat.

I turned back to Spenser.

"So how can we help you?" he said.

" '*We*'?" Hawk said. "Here we go."

I told them both, as quickly and as comprehensively as I could, everything that had happened since the pages and the knife had appeared in Melanie Joan's suite at The Newbury, through the murder of Richard Gross and my trip to Utica, all the way to the murder of Chaz Blackburn in his home on Ash Place. I concluded by telling them that if we didn't have a full-fledged serial killer at work here, we seemed to have one on training wheels.

Spenser took it all in. As he did, I saw him absently close the right-hand drawer to his new desk.

"Gun in there?" I said.

He nodded.

"I do the same thing when I don't know who's coming through the door," I said. "Even though I don't have Hawk."

"Who do?" Hawk said.

"I hear you've got a pretty solid wingman of your own," Spenser said.

"You know about Spike?" I said.

"Few don't," he said.

I drank more coffee. It was very good. Better than Keurig.

"I find myself in a situation," I said, "where I'm not sure I can protect everybody who might be in danger. And that's why I was hopeful that I might be able to hire you."

I asked what he charged. He told me.

I said, "Melanie Joan can afford it."

"I'm sure she can," Spenser said, "but in this case, it's irrelevant, because I'm heading out to Los Angeles on a case in the morning."

"Well, fuckety fuck," I said.

Spenser pushed the box of donuts in my direction.

"I forgot to offer you before," he said. "Pretty sure there's a couple cinnamons left. I can't speak for you. But donuts generally make me more optimistic about almost everything except the state of the union."

"Thanks," I said. "But I'm watching my figure."

"Same," Hawk said.

He smiled again.

I once again managed to maintain control.

"I made a few calls about you," Spenser said. "Just as a way of keeping myself sharp."

"Gonna take more than a few calls get *that* done," Hawk said.

"Heard that you've also been dealing with your father's problems with Joe Doyle," Spenser said.

"Which make them my problems," I said.

"Hence the need for reinforcements."

I grinned. "Hence."

Spenser said, "What about Vinnie Morris?"

"Texas," I said. "On a thing."

" 'Thing' with Vinnie can cover an expanse of territory as great as the Great Plains," Spenser said. "What about Tony Marcus?"

"All accounts between us are squared at the present time," I said. "I'd prefer to keep them that way."

"He mentioned to me when I last spoke to him that you owe him one."

"Pretty of him to think so," I said.

"Tony is one transactional son of a bitch," Spenser said.

"Aren't we all?" I said.

I picked up my mug and took it over to his sink and rinsed it, telling him Susan would be so proud.

"I'll figure something out," I said. "And it was nice to finally meet you."

Hawk sat up.

"Fuck Tony Marcus," he said. "And fuck Vinnie. I got this."

"Seriously?" I said.

"Already told Susan," he said.

"Thank you," I said to Hawk.

"You better off with me than my trusty sidekick, anyway," he said. "Case we got to cut a few corners."

"I thought you were the sidekick," Spenser said.

FORTY-SEVEN

Joe Doyle was seated in one of *my* client chairs when I got back to my office.

"I let myself in," he said.

"I can see that."

"You might think about better locks," he said. "And a better alarm system."

"See that, too."

I closed the door behind me and tossed my bag next to my desk and sat down. I told him I could make coffee. He said he wouldn't be here that long. I asked where his men were.

"Downstairs in the car," he said. "I told them you pose no threat to me."

"See what happens the next time you break into my office," I said.

He was wearing a vest today. I never got the vest thing with men, but there it was. Big shine to his cap-toed shoes. He was also wearing what I was willing to bet my rent was a Zegna print tie.

Joe Doyle. A man in full.

Giving off the general impression that somehow this was his office and not mine.

"What can I do for you, Mr. Doyle?" I said.

"Call me Joe."

"No, thanks."

"You're as hard as your father," he said.

"Not even on my best day," I said.

I excused myself and fired up my Keurig. I'd finished only half a cup at Spenser's office, even if his coffee *was* better.

"So what *can* I do for you?" I said when I sat back down.

"I'd like to hire you," he said.

Suddenly the private detective business in Boston had turned into a job fair.

I was wondering if there was a bad joke in here somewhere about throats being cut and cutthroat lawyers.

"You're kidding," I said.

"I have been accused of many things in my life, Ms. Randall," he said. "Being a great kidder has never been one of them."

"You threatened my father," I said. "You could have killed him having his car run off the road, even though I don't expect you'll ever admit to being behind that. And then, big finish, my father got shot saving your life."

266

I leaned forward in my chair, put my elbows on my desk, smiled at him, and said, "And now you want to *hire* me?"

"I've made my peace with your father," he said. "I might have misjudged him."

"No kidding," I said.

"He is more forgiving than you," Doyle said.

"The grudge-holding comes from my mother's side."

He crossed his legs, fussing with the crease on his top leg as he did. Then he stared down at those well-manicured hands. I wondered what the boys he'd grown up with in Southie would say about well-tended fingernails like those.

"You're not a lawyer," he said finally.

"And proud of it."

He grinned.

"What lawyers know," he said, "is that sometimes it's necessary to take emotion out of the equation with those they choose to defend. And we sure as *shite* don't have to like all of them. Or any of them. But often we do what we do, and not just for the money, because it happens to be the right thing to do."

Now I grinned, as I leaned back into my chair.

"You want to know what's a bunch of

shite, Mr. Doyle?" I said. *"That."*

"You know that the same person who shot at me and shot your father instead could have killed him as easily as he almost killed me," Doyle said. "And I believe the murder attempt has something to do with the death of my son. And might additionally have something to do with that cockroach John Melvin. And I have come to the conclusion that you are the best person to find that out."

"What a lucky girl am I," I said.

"You know I'm right."

"You *are* right," I said. "But I know you're aware that I've kind of got my hands full at the moment trying to keep Dr. Melvin's ex-wife alive."

"Your father explained that to me in the park," Joe Doyle said. "But he also explained that you'd been able to keep her safe while keeping him safe at the same time."

"Until I didn't," I said. "My father, I mean."

"The best-laid plans," Doyle said. "But I no longer pose any threat to him, either."

"Why in the world would I believe that?" I said.

"Because he did save my life," he said. "And I am now in his debt. It's a thing with the Irish."

268

"It's a thing with pretty much everybody."

His shoulder rose and fell as he took in a lot of air and let it out.

"I swear on my son's head that you can trust me on this," he said.

"Why didn't you tell me the first time we met that you had represented John Melvin?"

He smiled.

"Because it was none of your fucking business at the time," Doyle said.

There were a lot of things that came to mind in the moment. But with every lousy thing I was certain Joe Doyle had done in his life, what he'd *already* done to my father, he was talking about his dead son now. And even though I knew that the very best defense attorneys looked as if they'd been to acting school once they were playing to a courtroom, I couldn't bring myself to believe that the old man sitting across from me was that good an actor.

"I'll do it," I said.

"Good."

"Do you want to know what I charge?"

"I don't care."

"I can't promise I will give this matter my full attention until I roll up the other matter," I said.

"There's an Irish proverb covers that," he said. "*Tús maith, leath na hoibre.* A good

269

start is half the work. And I have the feel-ing, just the way you came at me when you came to *my* office, that half of you might be better than the total focus of a lesser man."

"Well," I said, "you'll get no argument from me on that."

Doyle said, "Someone went after my son, even in prison. But I think it was a way to get at me."

"Why you?"

"Because John Melvin blames me for still being behind bars, even if that is just another example of his madness," Doyle said. "He convinced himself that I would be the one to finally get him set free. I was quite willing to take his money. But I knew what all the other lawyers he'd hired knew before me: That he is going to die in prison."

"There's a proverb I often use that covers *that* one," I said. "Fuckin' ay."

Despite what he'd said about my alarm system, I knew moral alarms should be sounding for me, about him having worked for John Melvin as long as he did. But I chose to ignore them, at least for now.

I came back around my desk and put out my hand and he shook it, both of us look-ing the other in the eyes.

"You won't regret this," Joe Doyle said.

I already was. But felt that our budding

business relationship would get off to a bad start if I shared that with him.

FORTY-EIGHT

Spike said to Hawk, "I always wanted to be you when I grew up."

"Black and straight?" Hawk said.

"Well," Spike said, "the second piece would have been a deal-breaker."

"Shit people do for love," Hawk said. "Or don't."

Hawk sipped champagne. The bottle was next to him, at our table in the back room at Spike's. The only one drinking from it was Hawk. Spike and I were having martinis with extra olives. For this one night Melanie Joan was back at River Street Place with Richie and his son.

Takes a village.

When Richie had introduced her to the little boy, looking more and more like his father with each passing day, Melanie Joan had studied Richard as if he were some kind of extraterrestrial being.

As Richie had walked me to the door, he

said, "She doesn't appear to have had much experience with children."

"She considers herself an only child," I said, "in just about everything."

Now it was Spike and Hawk and me, attempting to format some kind of blueprint for keeping her safe. But I was already thinking that if Spike and Hawk and I couldn't manage that, my next call would have to be private militia.

Spike wore a white dress shirt and jeans and the new pair of Thursday boots he'd been bragging on. Hawk was wearing a black open-necked shirt and a pale gray suit that appeared to be just part of the general magnificent sculpture that was him.

I hadn't done any polling, but the vibe I was getting was that all of the women in the place wanted Hawk, and maybe half the guys. But my estimate could have been low with the guys.

I saw a young woman tall enough and pretty enough and in enough need of a hot meal to be a runway model excuse herself from the man with whom she was drinking at the bar and make her way directly toward Hawk.

In some kind of heavy European accent she said, "Didn't I see you at Fashion Week?"

273

" 'Course you did," Hawk said.

She asked if anybody at our table had a pen. Spike did. She took it from him and wrote her number down on a napkin. Old school.

"Call me," she said.

" 'Course I will," Hawk said.

She turned and walked back to the bar.

I said, "You ever been to Fashion Week?"

" 'Course I haven't," he said, and poured himself more champagne.

I reminded him again that he could pretty much name his own price with Melanie Joan. He reminded me again that he was giving her his flat rate.

"Tell me again what that is," I said.

"Soon as I come up with it," he said, "you be the first to know."

"Just be gentle," I said.

"Always am, missy," he said. "Always am."

Over dinner I had told him everything that had happened in more detail than I had at Spenser's office, everything I knew, everything I suspected. I shared that I was convinced that Melanie Joan knew more than she was telling. And I told him about John Melvin, and his connection to both Melanie Joan and Joe Doyle, and Doyle's connection to my father.

When I finished, Spike said, "So who

knows that Hawk's in this?"

"The three of us," I said. "Melanie Joan. Spenser and Susan Silverman. Richie. My dad. And I told Samantha Heller she might see Hawk on the perimeter from time to time."

"As a matter of fact, dear girl, she won't ever," Hawk said in a British accent.

"Sorry, Watson," I said.

He smiled again.

"Not your sidekick, either," he said.

I loved listening to him lapse in and out of street talk, the way Tony Marcus did. Tony had a lot more money, a lot more power, was a lot more streetwise, in all ways. But I knew enough about their relationship to know that Hawk was one of the few people in town, on either side of the line, to whom Tony always gave as much room as possible. Or just backed off entirely.

There was something else. Hawk was smarter than Tony, and not just street-smarter. He always got the joke, whatever the joke happened to be.

"You gonna need me to watch you some?" Hawk said to me. "Not like you not gonna be in the line of fire at some point."

"No," I said.

"Yes," Spike said.

"From what I see, over here on the perimeter you just spoke on," Hawk said, "is that somebody pickin' off people who've done good off Melanie Joan. And people she cares about, much as she's capable. We need to worry about the agent?"

"She says the protection Quill House, her agency, was willing to set up for Melanie Joan is easily transferred to her," I said.

"Not as good as us," Spike said. "And if you thought outside security was necessary, you would have asked for it in the first place."

Hawk said to Spike, "Just to be on the safe side, one of us ought to keep an eye on her time to time."

"Done," Spike said.

I said to Hawk, "Why are you doing this, really? We'd never even met until the other day."

"Thought I already explained that," he said. "When Susan Silverman tells me to jump, all's I generally asks is how high."

"Doesn't that reinforce hurtful racial stereotypes?" I said, grinning at him.

" 'Course it does," he said.

"What do we always hear about murder?" Spike said. "That the first two boxes to check are love and money."

"Before you get to the next one," Hawk said.

"And that would be?" Spike said.

"Hate," Hawk said. "You ask me, what we got goin' here is a different kind of hate crime, against a white girl writes books for a living."

FORTY-NINE

I sat in the same room as before with Dr. John Melvin. It was turning into our place.

Melvin acted as if he were even more delighted to see me this time.

"Finding out that you wanted to visit me again was such a pleasant surprise, Sunny," he said.

"*Visit* implies something social," I said. "For me, this is about as pleasant as seeing my OB/GYN."

He smiled.

"Does your ex-husband still find that bitch mouth of yours attractive?" he said.

"Endlessly," I said.

"I actually look at our verbal sparring as foreplay," Melvin said.

Now I smiled.

"Well, John," I said, "you're probably able to teach a master class in self-pleasuring."

He'd kept his beard trimmed and gotten another haircut since the last time I visited.

His old black-framed glasses were back.

"So what has brought us together again, other than destiny?" he said.

"Did you have someone try to kill Joe Doyle?"

"Now, that is such an interesting question," he said. "And makes me want to ask a couple questions of my own."

His voice was as soothing and melodious as ever. I imagined that the victims of his sexual assaults heard the same thing until the drugs he'd fed them began to kick in.

"My first question is why you think I would be involved in something as heinous as that with my old friend Joe?" he said. "And my second question goes something like this: Even if I *had* ordered a hit like that, why the *fuck* would I tell the person most responsible for me being in my current circumstances?"

I crossed my legs, carefully, because of the shortness of a skirt I had worn here for my own twisted amusement.

"Actually, John," I said, "the person most responsible for you being in your current circumstances, the result of being a sexual freak, is you."

"A debatable point," he said.

"Only if you're batshit crazy enough to actually believe that."

He sighed.

"All I know about someone taking a shot at Joe Doyle is what I've heard," he said.

"Who said somebody shot at him?"

Melvin shook his head.

"As I said, one hears things."

His pallor hadn't improved since the last time we'd been in this room together, to the point where it seemed to be the exact shade of his gray jumpsuit.

"Shame about your father getting caught in the crossfire," he said. "How's he doing?"

I ignored him.

"Joe Doyle says you continue to blame him for your most recent appeals being folded up into a party hat by the parole board," I said.

"Things might have been different if he'd put forth his best effort," Melvin said.

"I keep wondering," I said, "what would an actual therapist say about a blamer like you."

"Did you actually come here looking for some sort of full confession from me?" he said. "If so, we're going to be here awhile."

"They do say confession is good for the soul," I said. "But that presupposes that you have a soul."

"You know, Sunny," he said, "the way dead bodies keep popping up around you, maybe you should consider yourself fortunate that your father is still among the living."

I stared at him now. Even as we engaged in verbal cat-and-mouse, I never lost sight of the fact that he was both a monster and a predator.

"What sort of game are you playing here?" I said.

He seemed to brighten suddenly.

"Game?" he said. "Now, *that* would presuppose that there's only one, wouldn't it?"

He stood now, this aging jailhouse rat who still saw himself as some kind of dandy.

"You appear to have wasted today's drive out to Concord," he said.

"How so?"

"You wanted to find out if I had something to do with that man in black shooting your father," he said. "And I've disappointed you."

"Incidentally?" I said. "How'd you know the shooter was wearing black?"

He ignored me, started to shuffle toward the door. As the guard opened it for him, he stopped and turned back to me.

"I just worry sometimes that everything going on around my ex-wife," he said, "is just a lot of shiny-object misdirection, and that the person in the most danger here might be you, Sunny."

He laughed as the guard continued to hold the door open for him.

"I mean, wouldn't that be a plot twist worthy of the great Melanie Joan Hall?" he said.

Then he was gone.

And I wondered, not for the first time, who gave Dr. John Melvin the creeps.

FIFTY

On my way back to Boston I called Spike. He said he was at the restaurant, working on next week's staff schedule, but that Hawk was looking after Melanie Joan.

"So you gave the two of them a proper introduction," I said.

"So I did."

"And how did Melanie Joan, ah, react to him?"

Spike said, "Almost with a sense of wonder."

"Hawk must have found that amusing," I said.

"Just going off my limited exposure to him," Spike said, "Hawk would probably find a gun pointed at him amusing."

Samantha Heller was in Washington for a day. Before she'd left she told me that as impossible as it was for Melanie Joan to believe sometimes, she actually did have other clients. And now had one, a writer of spy thrillers, who needed some hand-holding, being so far past when the latest book should have been delivered that the publishing house was starting to act like the Mob, especially because the author's sales had dipped recently.

"Male or female?" I said.

She told me the name.

"Wait a second," I said. "You never told me you repped that hack."

"You never asked," she said. "And by the way? One girl's hack is another girl's big-assed earner."

"How does Melanie Joan feel when you have to devote your time and attention to another?" I said.

"How do you think?" Samantha said.

I told her my theory about Melanie Joan seeing herself as an only child.

"Bingo," Samantha Heller said.

"Somebody will be watching you even in our nation's capital?" I said.

"Every move I make," she said. "Every step I take."

I was taking the exit ramp off Storrow and considering calling Richie Burke and asking him to dinner if he could get a babysitter on short notice when Holly Hall called to tell me that her husband had died.

FIFTY-ONE

Two days later I drove back to Whitesboro, New York, not so much to pay my respects to the widow Hall, but curious to see how many of his former female students would show up for his memorial service.

Particularly women, as they say, of a certain age.

"I had this friend," Tom Gorman said to me outside the church, "who used to get around pretty good when he was young. With the ladies, I mean."

"Ladies?" I said. "I thought that word had finally fossilized."

Gorman grinned.

"Anyway," he said, "one time I pointed out to this guy what a bad boyfriend he'd always been. And you know what he said? 'Tommy, someday they'll all put roses on my casket.' "

"What kind of boyfriend are you?" I said.

"Great!" Gorman said. "I can show you,

you want."

The Whitesboro Presbyterian Church *was* mostly filled with women, of all ages. It wasn't a particularly long service. The pastor, who looked as old as Charles Hall had been, spoke briefly. Holly Hall spoke lovingly of her late husband, stopping a few times to compose herself.

At one point she paused and looked out at the congregation and said, "I forget where I read this, but it describes my husband perfectly. He was a good man, and a very bad boy."

She paused again.

"Charles loved two things above all other," Holly said. "He loved words, and he loved women."

She smiled.

"In no particular order," she said. "And I must tell you, as his wife, that I did find myself wishing he had loved words a little more and women a little less."

And got a big, knowing laugh inside Whitesboro Presbyterian.

Tom Gorman and I were standing in back. He quietly began to sing as the organ music came up at the end.

" 'Of all the girls I loved before . . .' " he sang.

"No respect for the dead?" I said.

He grinned.

"From everything I've now learned about this guy," Gorman said, "and even as old as he was, I'm shocked he didn't die in the saddle."

After Holly had traveled to the cemetery with the casket, she had arranged for a gathering in the gymnasium at the college. I planned to stay for that, and then drive home, having not even booked a hotel room for the night.

I didn't know exactly what I expected to learn here, or from whom. But it defied both logic and common sense — neither strong suits of mine — that if someone had written the original version of *A Girl and Not a God,* she had to have been a student of Charles Hall's back in the day, around the time both Melanie Joan and Holly had been trying to score more than good grades.

Tom Gorman and I grabbed plastic glasses of soft seltzer water and stood against the boarded-up bleachers, watching the church crowd slowly begin to reassemble.

"What you are lucky enough to be witnessing," he said, "is the rock-solid foundation of my journalistic career."

"And what would that be?"

"Lean against a wall and hope something interesting develops," he said.

287

Holly Hall arrived a few minutes later.

As soon as she set foot inside the gym, one of the women of a certain age slapped her.

FIFTY-TWO

The woman who slapped her looked to be roughly the same age, and even the same height, as Holly.

Long, straight hair, a deft combination of blond and gray. Her black dress fit her beautifully. Low heels. Simple strand of pearls.

I had to admit, the closer I got, the better she looked. Tom Gorman and I moved quickly across the gym floor. Somehow everybody else in their immediate area had backed away, but not far enough that they might miss whatever was going to happen next.

Holly Hall's cheek was pink where the woman had connected.

"Problem?" I said when Gorman and I got to them.

"Who are you?" the woman said. "Another one of Charlie's angels?"

"I'm actually just waiting for cake," I said.

"Is that supposed to be funny?" the woman said.

I turned to Tom Gorman, who seemed to be enjoying the show even more now that I was in it.

"When they have to ask," I said sadly.

"I've got this, Sunny," Holly said.

She turned back to the woman wearing a black dress that I could now confirm, up close to it, had not been purchased in a department store.

"Please don't make more of a scene than you already have," Holly said to her.

"I've actually done everything I came here to do," the woman said. "And I wanted to let you know that if you thought I'd forgotten your betrayal, you are sadly, and perhaps pathetically, lying to yourself. But then, you were always such an artful liar, Holly."

"Lisa," Holly said. "Please lower your voice."

Lisa smiled.

"Unlike you, dear," she said, "this is as low as I go."

I stuck out my hand to Lisa, hoping to somehow shift her attention, and de-escalate the situation at the same time.

"Sunny Randall," I said, as if on the welcoming committee for orientation.

She looked down at my hand, then back at me.

"Who gives a shit?" she said.

I smiled and stepped a little closer to her, now that she had officially annoyed me.

"Lisa," I said, "this is probably the first and last time we will ever encounter each other. I'm a private detective, and have a gun in my purse, which actually isn't relevant to this conversation. But this is: Rude people annoy me. And now you have. So if you don't leave this gym right now, I am going to stick your elbow in your ear."

It was a line from Spenser that Susan Silverman had once shared with me. I'd been saving it for a special occasion. This was it.

Lisa stared at me. Opened her mouth and closed it. This close to her, I saw that her eyes were so pale that they were almost translucent.

"You can't talk to me like that," she said.

"Just did, hon," I said.

"This is between Holly and me," she said.

"Was," I said.

"Sunny," Holly said, "please let me handle this before the entire occasion is ruined."

I ignored her. When I got closer to Lisa now, she took a step back, almost involuntarily.

I leaned in now and whispered, "Don't

make *me* slap *you.*"

I turned to Tom Gorman and winked.

I turned back to Lisa the bitch and said, "Now, for the last time, turn around and get your skinny ass out of here."

And she did.

FIFTY-THREE

"Her name is Lisa Karlin," Holly said. "She was in Melanie Joan's class. As besotted by Charles as we all were, and we were in competition for him, which he enjoyed thoroughly. It was part of his mystique, that the names of the girls would change, but the fighting over him never did."

She shook her head.

"I sometimes thought it was as exciting for him as having sex with us," she said.

We were back at the cottage by now, just the two of us. Tom Gorman had gone back to the paper to write his column about Charles Hall, after marveling at the way I'd run off Lisa Karlin.

"Let's skip you finding out what a great boyfriend and fun date I am and just get married," he said when I walked him to his car.

"No," I said.

"Why not?" he said. "Am I punching

above my weight?"

"Little bit."

Holly asked if I wanted a drink. I told her I was leaving from here for Boston. She was still talking, almost as much for her benefit as mine, about the romantic life and times of the late Dr. Charles Hall.

"I don't mean to speak ill of the dead," I said, "and I know he was your husband, but he sounds like a predator to me."

"I can see how you'd think that way," she said. "But it was never an Epstein-type situation. It was almost like it was part of taking his course."

"Sounds quite romantic."

"You're being sarcastic."

"You *think*?" I said.

"I'm not explaining it well," she said.

"Unfortunately," I said, "you're doing just fine."

"It was just a different time," she said. "A different world. Even looking back, it seems quite innocent to the nineteen-year-old me."

"Sounds like he should have been teaching a course in daddy issues," I said.

She had poured herself vodka over ice. She drank some of it.

"So all this time later, why does Lisa Karlin show up and give you a good smack?" I said.

"She's still accusing me of stealing one of her stories," Holly said, "as a way of ingratiating myself with Charles."

"Did you?"

"No!" Holly Hall said. "I was never going to be a good enough writer to catch his eye like that. But she thought she was. A writer, I mean. Only at that time he only had eyes for Melanie Joan. He dumped me for her. Maybe Lisa thought if she wrote well enough he'd dump Melanie Joan for her. But it never happened. Because she couldn't write well enough."

"Could Melanie Joan have stolen someone like Lisa Karlin's work?" I said. "Is it possible that's the secret that Charles kept for her?"

"I guess anything is possible," she said. "All I know is that at the time he had convinced himself that Melanie Joan was going to be a star, and that he was going to be known as the man who discovered her. One time he was reading aloud from another magazine story about her in which she said she never could have made it without him. And he said, 'People don't know the half of it.'"

"But he didn't explain."

She shook her head.

"She talked about him as if he had some

sort of power over her," Holly said. "And who knows? Maybe he did."

Melanie Joan had married two controlling men. Her English professor and her therapist. Maybe if Richard Gross had dumped his wife for Melanie Joan and become her third husband, he would have fit the profile, too.

Holly finished her drink. I could tell she wanted another, and knew she'd have one as soon as I was out the door, and then another after that.

"So many memories today," she said. "Good and bad. Maybe it was Lisa confronting me the way she did that triggered them even more vividly."

"Hard to believe she still hasn't gotten over not making the cut after all these years," I said.

Holly sighed.

"At least she didn't kill herself over him," she said.

"Excuse me?" I said.

"It's someone I hadn't thought about in years and years," Holly said. "Another one who didn't make the cut, as they say, even before Melanie Joan and Lisa and I came along. Another one who thought *she* was going to be one of Charlie's literary angels."

"Do you have a name?" I said.

She told me that as a matter of fact she did.

FIFTY-FOUR

I was about two hours into the ride back, just crossing over into Massachusetts on the turnpike, when Tom Gorman called.

"I'm starting to feel a connection here," he said. "You must be feeling it, too."

"Lie down," I said. "I'm certain it will pass."

"As we continue to get to know each other," he said, "you'll start to look more favorably upon my persistence."

"We're not going to continue to know each other," I said.

I looked in the rearview mirror, saw myself smiling. I liked him. But that was for me to know.

"You asked me for help, remember," he said.

"So I did," I said. "Must have slipped my mind in all the excitement of the day."

He had already managed to do a lot with what Holly Hall had told me about the young woman named Jennifer Price. She had enrolled at Whitesboro College a couple years before Holly had. She had taken Charles Hall's writing seminar her second semester junior year.

She had not, Gorman informed me, come back for her senior year.

"But I'm burying the lead," he said. "For which I apologize."

"Accepted," I said.

"Two years after Jennifer Price would have graduated," Gorman said, "she was found dead in the house she'd been renting in New Ashford, Massachusetts, where she'd been working as an assistant librarian."

"How did she die?"

"Slit her wrists in the bathtub," he said.

He didn't say anything right away. Neither did I.

Finally he said, "Let me tell you what else I got, not that it's a hell of a lot."

He said that in what little coverage of her death he could find, there was no next of kin listed, the one obit he'd read in the Springfield paper saying that both of her parents were dead. She was single, according to the obit, and had been living in a cabin in the woods.

"The only quote in the story," Gorman said, "was from the head librarian, now deceased. She described Jennifer Price as a sweet, fragile creature of this earth who loved books as much as anybody she'd ever met."

"Once you learned the librarian had passed away, you called the town," I said.

"Cops in and around small towns know a lot of stuff," he said.

"What about the library?"

"No one working there now was working there then," he said. "It's not like you're dealing with the Boston Public Library. It appears to be a pretty small operation, then and now."

"Thank you for doing this," I said.

"You're welcome," he said. "You want me to keep digging?"

"Just to keep the connection between us strong," I said.

"You said there wasn't a connection."

"I might have spoken in haste."

"Should we think there might possibly be a connection in the long-ago between Jennifer Price and Melanie Joan Hall?" Gorman said.

"Why not?" I said.

FIFTY-FIVE

Melanie Joan told me she wanted to hear everything about the memorial service, not to leave anything out. I'd spent two hours on the Mass Pike at a dead stop because of a tractor-trailer accident, and I was too tired right now for show-and-tell.

So I gave her a drive-thru version of the service and the scene in the gym. She said that she was sorry she'd missed what she called the bitch-off between Holly and Lisa. I told her I would elaborate tomorrow on an early-morning walk before the breakfast we'd scheduled with Samantha Heller, said good night to Spike before he left, poured myself a glass of Jameson, carried it and Rosie toward the stairs.

Even the conversation I wanted to have with her about the late Jennifer Price could wait until morning, when I expected to be far more alert than I presently was.

"I just want to leave you with one

thought," Melanie Joan said when I was halfway up the stairs. "Not only did Holly Hall hate me, she hated all of us."

"Define *us*," I said.

"All of us who were just as pretty as she was and *way* more talented, dear," she said.

"I will keep that in mind," I said.

"And by the way?" Melanie Joan continued. "She was the most jealous person I've ever known."

I went upstairs, took a long, hot shower, did my brushing of teeth and hair and creaming of my face. But when I did get into bed, I dialed Holly Hall's cell phone, not to share Melanie Joan's withering assessment of her, but to ask a couple more questions about Jennifer Price.

I went straight to voicemail on the cell, then dialed the landline.

A woman answered.

"This is Sunny Randall," I said. "To whom am I speaking?"

"This is Meg," the woman said. "I was one of Charles's caretakers."

"Is Holly okay?" I said.

I was beginning to test high on paranoia.

"Oh, she's perfectly fine," Meg said. "She just decided on the spur of the moment, or so she said, to get away for a few days, and asked me to stay with the dog."

"I wasn't aware they had a dog," I said.

"Some dogs bark when there are visitors," Meg said. "Sammy generally hides under the bed."

"I tried her cell," I said. "She didn't pick up."

"It's because the phone is right here on the kitchen table," Meg said. "Holly said she was going rogue while she was away."

"If she checks in with you," I said, "would you tell her that I called?"

She said she would.

"You're the private investigator, right?" Meg said.

"That is I."

"Did you find what you came here looking for?" Meg said.

"Not so's you'd notice," I said.

In the morning, a few minutes after six, Melanie Joan and I were on our morning walk, undeterred when we stepped outside and a light rain began to fall. As it did, I stared up into a sky that was the color of pewter.

"It doesn't look good up there," I said to her.

"You're not weaseling out on me because of a little rain," she said. "Trust me. Someday when you're my age, it will take more than rain to keep you from your appointed rounds."

I grinned at her as I did some brief stretching.

"And what age is that, exactly?" I said.

"You continue to be not as funny as you think you are," Melanie Joan said.

"I know," I said sadly. "Oh, don't I know."

Then she announced we were going all the way to the Harvard Bridge, which she assured me was not going to be a bridge too far today. That if she were feeling it, we might make two trips to the bridge instead of one.

"Oh, joy," I said.

And as we started off at a fairly brisk pace, I took her through the memorial service more fully than I had the night before. She was thrilled all over again to hear that Lisa Karlin had slapped Holly, and now chastised me for coming to Holly's defense.

Melanie Joan said, "Lisa was another of his no-talent cuties."

She turned her head slightly and said, "And before you make one of your smart comments, just remember that I was a cutie *with* talent. And have the sales to prove it."

We walked in silence then for a few minutes until I said, "Why *were* you so generous with Charles Hall?"

"Did you ever date an older man?" she said.

"How old?"

"More than twice your age," she said.

"No," I said. "I was a fine arts major. But I could also count."

"Looking back," she said, "it may appear to you that Charles was using me. But the fact of things is that we were using each other."

Now I turned and saw her frowning, as if conducting some interior debate about what to say next.

Or how much to say next.

"Another fact of things is that I could not have finished the first draft of that first novel without him," she said. She hesitated, if briefly, and continued. "On so many different levels. There's no book without him, even though the finished product was vastly different. And far better. He wasn't much of a writer, and was honest enough with himself to know that. But he could turn someone like me into one. On that he was quite convincing, and persuasive." She lifted her shoulders and dropped them. "So I slept with him. And then later I married him. Looking back, I almost think of myself as a literary courtesan."

I grinned.

305

"Courtesan," I said. "Not a word that pops up in conversation normally."

"It does if the conversations are in my books," she said.

We walked another couple hundred yards in silence, the rain beginning to pick up now, but we were close enough to the bridge that it was silly to turn back yet.

"Holly said that he never told her whatever it was that you didn't want disclosed," I said. "And which, I might point out, you've never disclosed to me."

"I told you," she said. "The money was my way of giving him his proper credit for the boost he gave me. But it was my insurance that he wouldn't take too much credit."

"And he never talked."

"He wouldn't," she said. "He was the most gentlemanly man who ever violated all the norms about teachers and students, as contradictory as that might sound."

"You want my honest opinion about that?" I said.

"Is there any other kind with you?" she said.

"It doesn't just sound contradictory, it sounds like happy horseshit," I said. "Charles Hall was a skeevy old man even before he was old."

"I'm still sorry he's dead," she said. "And

306

that he had such a sad ending."

"I'd hoped he might be able to help us figure all of this out," I said.

"So had I," Melanie Joan said, with what I thought sounded like a thrilling lack of conviction.

"Tell me about Jennifer Price," I said then.

She briefly stopped and turned to look at me.

"Now, there's a name I haven't heard in over thirty years," she said. She grinned. "Or closer to forty, depending on who's doing the counting."

When we were walking again, I told her that I knew Jennifer Price had arrived at Whitesboro College before she did, and left early.

"When Charles did reference her," Melanie Joan said, "he did so almost with melancholy, even before he learned of her passing. I remember one time, after he'd had too much wine, when he talked about how he had failed her."

We had reached the bridge by now and were turning around. The rain came harder. There had been light traffic on the Esplanade on our way up here, from runners and walkers. But now the morning had gone almost completely dark, the path had emptied out, and we had no choice but to soldier our way back home.

"You want to run?" I shouted over the storm.

"No," she said. "But let's pick up the pace."

We ducked our heads. The wind off the river was blowing directly at us now.

It was why I didn't see the bike speeding toward us until it was about fifty yards away, and the rider was raising his gun.

I heard the sound of the gunshot quite clearly over the storm and shoved Melanie Joan to the side of the path as the shooter stopped the bike now and let it fall to the ground and took a couple steps in our direction.

He raised his gun, firing again, missing again as I rolled in front of Melanie Joan, reaching down for the .38 I had in the side pocket of my rain jacket. I knew the snubnose wasn't going to do much good for me from this distance. But I got myself into a kneeling position now, saw that there were no pedestrians behind the guy, returned fire anyway.

The man, dressed all in black, was silhouetted against the river behind him.

Like the black ninja my father had described, the one who had shot at Joe Doyle and shot my father instead.

308

Red bike.

He fired two more shots through the wind and rain and howl of the morning. I'd emptied my gun by now. But unless he'd been counting, he had no way of knowing that.

Somehow I heard the first siren in the distance, then saw him pick his bike up and get on and head back in the direction from which he'd come.

I briefly thought about sprinting after him.

Not with an empty gun.

So I just stood there and watched the bicycle disappear into the storm until it was completely out of view.

FIFTY-SIX

After I'd finished giving my report about the shooting to the police on the scene, I went back to my office. Joe Doyle showed up a half-hour later, saying he wanted to pay me in person as he handed me a rather impressive check.

"I didn't do anything to earn this," I said.

"Your father did."

"Pay him."

"He didn't want my money, Ms. Randall," Doyle said. "Are you now telling me that my money isn't good enough for you, either?"

The check sat on my desk in front of me.

"I generally only get paid for services rendered," I said. "I honestly believe that in this case, the renderer was my pops."

Joe Doyle smiled thinly. Perhaps it was all he had in him. I told him what had just happened along the Charles. He nodded. In all likelihood, he already knew about it.

"Take the win," he said. "Going forward, I will determine who put out the hit on me. And on the two of you this morning, if it's the same person. And deal with it accordingly."

There was no point in asking what "accordingly" meant. It would have been like asking Tony Marcus.

"Do you think it's John Melvin?" I said.

Another thin smile.

"I believe I'll invoke my Fifth Amendment rights here," he said. "As a way of protecting myself from self-incrimination."

"Anyone who knows me knows that I don't believe in coincidence," I said.

"Who the fuck does?" Joe Doyle said.

"Let me ask you something," I said. "Do you believe that Melvin had something to do with Joe Jr.'s death?"

"For the sake of conversation," he said, "what would it matter to you if I did?"

"You're still technically my client," I said. "Information is power."

"Just know this," Doyle said. "If something ever does happen to Melvin, and his death isn't of natural causes, then the world will be a far better place without him. That *I* know. What we still don't know, either one of us, is who that shooter was." He leaned back in the client chair and clasped his

311

hands on his chest. "But when it comes to getting even, Ms. Randall, I've always played the long game."

I thought: *Who doesn't these days?*

He stood now.

"You and your father can decide what to do with the money," he said. "If you consider it blood money, then just tear it up."

He came around my desk. Now I stood. He put out his hand. I shook it.

"Pleasure doing business with you," he said.

"Don't take this the wrong way," I said. "But I wish I could say the same."

He walked out then, gently closing the door behind him.

A few hours later I was walking back to River Street Place with Richie, after the two of us had lunched at Stephanie's on Newbury, when the hospital in Concord called to inform me that this time John Melvin was the one who had been shanked in the yard, and might not make it.

FIFTY-SEVEN

The doctor, whose name tag read *Herre,* said, "He's really too weak to have visitors. But he was insistent that I contact you."

"Is he dying?" I said.

"Are you family?"

"Hardly."

"All I can tell you is that he lost a lot of blood," Dr. Herre said. "And he doesn't appear to have a lot of wellness on which to fall back."

"John Melvin," Richie said, "is a wellness-free zone."

Richie had insisted on coming with me. He said that if Melvin really was about to kick, he didn't want to miss it. Richie hadn't forgotten Melvin's plan to drug and rape me before he burst through the door that day with his gun in his hand. Joe Doyle had talked about playing the long game with getting even. But maybe it hadn't turned out to be a long game at all between Doyle and Melvin.

"He may pull out of this," Dr. Herre said.

"Pity," Richie said.

"You sound like your father," I said to him.

"Comes and goes," he said.

The version of John Melvin I saw today was like some old article of clothing that had faded so much over time you could no longer recall its original color. His glasses were on the table next to the bed. He seemed to have dozed off before Dr. Herre walked Richie and me in.

He opened his eyes, and actually smiled when he saw me. But the smile vanished as quickly as it had appeared when he saw Richie standing next to me.

"What's he doing here?" Melvin said in a weak voice not much more than a whisper.

Richie said, "If this really is it, Melvin, I didn't want to miss the grand finale. And the happy ending."

"Said the gangster's son," Melvin said.

"To the psycho therapist," Richie said.

Melvin adjusted his head on the pillow just enough to focus his attention on me. Somehow he seemed two sizes too small. Like the Grinch's heart. Except that even the Grinch turned out to have a heart. I wondered, certainly not for the first time, how Melanie Joan had managed to capture something that was never really there.

I had already mentioned to John Melvin that I didn't believe he had a soul.

"Why did you want to see me?" I said to him.

"Perhaps to make things right between us while I still can?" he said.

I heard Richie make a snorting noise.

"Did you send somebody to shoot at me and your ex?" I said.

"Wouldn't you like to know," Melvin said.

"The shooter was dressed the same way as the one who shot at Joe Doyle and hit my father," I said. "On the same red bike."

"What are the odds?" Melvin said.

He laughed softly, but the sound quickly devolved into coughing that contorted his face into pain, and was almost as painful to hear.

When the coughing ended he somehow managed to smile again. "Now, the shooting in the park," he said, "*does* sound like something that might have appealed to me. But that's ground we've covered before, haven't we, Sunny?"

I said, "Joe Doyle is of the additional belief that you might have had something to do with his son's death."

"If he is still wondering about that after I'm gone," Melvin said, "that would be my own sweet revenge."

So much of that going around, I thought.

"I'm curious about something," Richie said now. "Just how much revenge have you been looking for from in here? You can't possibly hate Joe Doyle as much as you hate your ex-wife. Or my ex-wife, for that matter. Or me."

Melvin raised his head slightly, as if to study Richie more closely, like an old patient, perhaps.

Even now, with what little strength he clearly had left, he seemed to be enjoying himself. Like a kid who didn't want the game to end.

"What are you asking me, really?" he said to Richie. "Did I hire someone to kill people close to Melanie Joan? And then expand the perimeter, I guess you could call it, to include someone as close to Sunny as her father? It's interesting to ponder, isn't it? Maybe the first shooter was supposed to take out both Joe Doyle and poor old Phil Randall that day, and would have, until Phil started shooting back."

"I'm supposed to believe you didn't send the same guy after Melanie Joan and me?" I said.

"Believe whatever you want, Sunny," he said. "It keeps the magic and mystery alive in our relationship."

"You have no fucking relationship with her," Richie said.

Melvin started coughing again, the sound even louder and rheumier than before, to the point where I was surprised Dr. Herre didn't come through the door.

"You need to rest," I said to John Melvin.

"When I'm dead," Melvin said. And winked. "Warren Zevon."

Richie said, " 'Poor Pitiful Me.' "

"I'm sorry?" Melvin said.

"Another Zevon song that could have been about you."

Melvin looked at me again.

"Has it occurred to you, Sunny," he said, "that maybe somebody just wanted you to *think* I'd sent the second shooter?"

He motioned me closer and whispered, "Just know that someday all of your questions about me will be answered."

He closed his eyes then. A minute later he was snoring softly.

Melanie Joan, the closest Melvin had to next of kin, got the call a little after ten o'clock from Dr. Herre telling her that after Richie and I had left his room, Dr. John Melvin had never regained consciousness.

317

Now both of Melanie Joan's ex-husbands were dead. And her boyfriend. And her editor.

It didn't take any kind of great detective to observe that the men in her life were dropping like flies.

FIFTY-EIGHT

"People keep dying," I said to Hawk.

"You don't miss nothin' now, do you?"

"What I'm mostly doing," I said, "is spinning my wheels."

"Like that Peloton," Hawk said. "Workin' your ass off and goin' nowhere. Never could understand that shit."

"Feel the burn," I said.

" 'Feel the *burn*'?" he said. "You really want to sound older than Jane Fonda?"

We were drinking in the bar at The Newbury, which we both still called the old Ritz. Hawk had ordered a $200 bottle of Taittinger. I was drinking Bushmills neat. My father was babysitting Melanie Joan. She was probably developing a crush on him at this point. All women, of all ages, did eventually.

Hawk was wearing a double-breasted navy blazer, a white V-neck T-shirt underneath, gray jeans, and black cowboy boots. We were at the table centered at the window facing out onto Arlington Street and the Public Garden.

I told him I'd been with Susan earlier in the day.

"Means you smarter than when you woke up this morning," he said. "Always a good thing."

"Isn't it, though," I said.

"People always be talkin' about class this and class that," Hawk said. "Only two classes of people that matter, you ask me. There's the class tryin' to smarten the world up, and every asshole tryin' to dumb it down."

"Lately I am feeling as if I belong to the second class," I said. I grinned. "Second-class citizen in all ways."

" 'Cause you ain't figured it all out yet, like you think you should. Spenser gets the same way."

"The bodies do keep piling up," I said. "The only one dead by natural causes is the professor."

"You more worried about Doyle getting Melvin done?" Hawk said. "Or who else Melvin might've *gotten* done?"

"It was interesting," I said to Hawk, "that as much as he wanted me to think he was masterminding everything, he wouldn't cop to sending the shooter after Melanie Joan and me."

"Sounds to me like the old fuck lived to play his damn games," Hawk said.

"Or die playing them."

"You believe him?"

"No."

"Two people close to Miss Mellie get they throats cut," Hawk said. "Even I don't run into a lot of that."

"Same," I said.

I sipped some whiskey. Hawk poured himself more champagne. I had already seen him drink an entire bottle at Spike's, and that had no discernible effect on him. Other than immediately making him order another bottle.

"I go back to the beginning," I said to Hawk. "Somebody wanted to torture Melanie Joan."

" 'Fore they kilt her."

"But when somebody did come after *her*," I said, "it was with a gun and not a knife."

"Hard to get near enough with a knife with all of us stayin' close like we are to that old ass of hers," he said.

"She's pretty proud of that ass," I said. "And I actually think she looks pretty good back there."

"Only a practiced eye like my own would

notice gravity starting to do its thang on her."

I grinned.

"That settles it," I said. "I'm walking behind you when we leave."

We drank for a few moments in silence. Hawk occupied himself smiling at a tall redhead at the bar. Up to now, *she* had remained clothed.

"Who's got the most skin in the game?" Hawk said.

"That much hasn't changed," I said. "Whoever thinks they had a book stolen from them."

"Yowza," Hawk said.

"Sounds like the money is about to be cut off with the widow Hall," I said.

"Maybe you need to have another talk with her," Hawk said.

"I'll put her on my list."

He smiled again. The only time he changed expression was when he smiled. But it was worth the wait, every time. Now the redhead at the bar knew.

I said, "I keep thinking it has to be more than just Susan asking for you to help me like this."

"No," he said. "It don't."

He paused and said, "Other than me being bored."

"You couldn't take a vacation?"

"Not alone," he said. "And I is, as they say, currently between engagements."

He nodded at the bar.

"Though that could be about to change," he said. "Im-i-nent-ly."

"Look at you," I said. "About to make a new friend."

" 'Fore I go, listen up," he said. "You do what you got to do and not worry about Miss Mellie. Me and the Pink Panther got this."

I smiled now, fully.

"Spike know you call him that?"

"Sho' nuff," Hawk said. "He can't be the Black Panther, on account of that bein' me."

"Four people dead in this thing," I said.

Hawk winked at me.

"Check your math, you get home," he said.

He waved for the check and signed it and told me he could walk me home. But I knew he didn't mean that, and so did he.

"You like redheads?" I said.

"Like all of what you call your woman-kind," he said.

And then he was heading for the bar.

I let him go first. No way I was letting him talk about my butt the way he talked about Melanie Joan's.

FIFTY-NINE

Melanie Joan was asleep when I got back to River Street Place. My father was watching a *Blue Bloods* rerun in the living room.

"I think Tom Selleck is trying to look more like Theodore Roosevelt with that mustache and those little glasses," he said. "You know Roosevelt was the first police commissioner in New York, right?"

"I do know that," I said. "And I liked Selleck much better when he was Magnum."

"You were too young when the old *Magnum* was on," Phil Randall said, in the early stages of an exhaustive search for his car keys.

"When they're as cute as he was," I said, "age is just a number."

I picked his car keys up off the sofa, hugged him, and said, "And when they're as cute as you are."

I walked Rosie, double-checked all the doors and windows on the ground floor

324

when we got back, Rosie having success-
fully neighborhood-watched again. Then I
picked Rosie up, dropped her off in my bed,
and continued up to my studio, where I had
spent hardly any time at all on my painting
lately.

Art, I had explained to Spike the other
day, always suffered when you were trying
to figure shit out.

"I think I read where Monet said that one
time," he said.

Melanie Joan and Samantha Heller were
on their way to New York City in a couple
days for meetings with publishers ready and
willing to throw money at her and try to get
her to switch houses now that Chaz Blackburn was gone.

The plan was for Spike to take them to
Logan Airport whenever they decided to
leave. The Quill House had arranged to have
two ex-NYPD guys they used sometimes
for their most important authors to meet
them at LaGuardia and take them to the
Peninsula Hotel, where they would share a
suite. Melanie Joan would audition the
publishers in the same suite, they'd fly
home, Spike would meet them at the airport.

"By which time," Samantha said, "the ka-
chinging will start."

"Is that a literary expression?" I asked her.

"I think Dickens was the first to use it," she said.

I hadn't used an easel in years, having discovered what talent I had was better suited to watercolors. But there was an easel set up in the studio just in case I changed my mind and got tired of working flat.

The canvas was blank, as it had been since the day I'd bought the easel. I grabbed a Magic Marker from the desk, and set about making one of my world-class lists. I almost always write these lists on yellow legal pads. But tonight I was hopeful that with a much bigger blank page, one I was in the process of un-blanking, I might somehow bring more clarity to the big picture.

That was the plan, anyway.

Once more I went back to the beginning, the first chapter of the ghost book being delivered to Melanie Joan. Then I went through everything that had happened in Boston since, all the way to Melanie Joan and me being shot at.

Everything that had happened in Whitesboro.

My visits to John Melvin at MCI-Concord, which always sounded as if *it* should be the name of a cop show.

Had he been trying to get even with

everyone he thought had wronged him before somebody got even with him?

Or had he been lying to the bitter end?

In a separate column I named the dead, in formation.

Richard Gross
Chaz Blackburn
Charles Hall
Melvin

Then I remembered what Hawk had said before he was presumably off for a night of heavenly transport.

Or some such.

"Check your math," he'd said.

And I realized I had left off one name.

The next morning Spike was at the house bright and early and I was back in my car, on my way to New Ashford, Massachusetts, where Jennifer Price had once lived, and died.

SIXTY

To get to New Ashford you got off 90 not long after you passed Pittsfield. Waze said the trip would take two hours and forty-two minutes. I made it in two and a half. That would show them.

In the last census of New Ashford I could find, there were fewer than three hundred people living in what was described as the third-smallest town in Berkshire County. I wondered what the population was in the two that were smaller.

There was a town government, but no schools, children in New Ashford being bused to two adjacent towns. You constantly heard the expression about postcard New England towns. This one really was about the size of one. I was pleasantly surprised that there was a library. But there it was, a small, two-story building, down the street from the Purple Pub, not far from the Liberty Market and the cannabis store. With three hundred people living here, I assumed there was enough cannabis in there to get the whole town high.

I had booked a room at the New Ashford Motor Inn for the night, the place more like a small country inn, stopping there just long enough to throw down my bag before setting out to discover what I could discover about Jennifer Price, now dead since the 1980s. I figured that if I went door-to-door asking about her, I could cover the whole town in two days. Three, tops.

I started at the library. I loved libraries, had since I was a little girl. I hadn't been very excited the first time my father had taken me to a ballgame at Fenway Park. But I could still remember the sense of wonder, the kind he'd wanted me to get from baseball, the first time he'd walked me into the Boston Public Library on Boylston Street.

And I'd spent a lot of my growing-up years in the stacks of the Newton Free Library. Phil Randall had always called all libraries capitals for dreamers.

Now I felt the same quiet magic at this place in New Ashford. The head librarian's desk was right in front of me as I walked in. Her nameplate read *Margaret Thompson.*

I introduced myself and handed her one of my cards. She smiled.

"I'll trade you a library card for one of those business cards," she said.

"Only if you promise it will make me smarter," I said.

"They always do," Margaret Thompson said.

"I feel as if I may be tilting at windmills here," I said.

She smiled again. Not a customer smile.

"Well, then," she said, "you've come to the right place."

I asked if she had ever heard the name Jennifer Price. She said she had not. I told her the sad story of Jennifer Price's life and death, and when she would have worked at the library.

"That would have been when Katherine Baum was head librarian, not long after they decided to open this place," Margaret Thompson said. "She was a bit of a local legend, still working here when she passed at the age of eighty-five."

"I don't suppose you have any sort of digital record on employees in the time she worked here," I said.

Margaret Thompson laughed.

"Oh, wait," she said. "You were serious."

"The only reason I know she worked here at all," I said, "is because Katherine Baum was quoted in the obit about her we dug up in the Springfield paper."

"I wish I could help you more," Margaret Thompson said. "But I didn't come to work here until twenty years after you say Miss Price died."

I had printed a copy of the obit and took it out of my bag and put it on her desk. Margaret Thompson read it.

"Mrs. Baum is gone and Jennifer is gone," she said. "And I mean long gone."

"Maybe Town Hall would have further information about her," she said. "Tax records or something like that. I'm fumbling here." I grinned. "One of my many specialties."

"Did I pass the Town Hall on my way here from the motor lodge?" I said.

"It's on Seven," she said, "past us. Not more than a five-minute drive. But then nothing much in New Ashford is more than five minutes away."

"Is there a local police department where somebody might pull up the file on Jennifer Price's death?" I asked, having not seen one mentioned in my limited research on New Ashford.

"Cheshire," she said.

I thanked her for her time, and for doing God's work as a librarian, and went out to the car and called the paper in Springfield,

331

known as *The Republican.* I asked if there was any chance that Dan Fimrite, who'd gotten the byline on Jennifer Price's obit, still worked there. The woman who answered the phone said that Mr. Fimrite had died in 2009.

I drove over to Town Hall, a building even smaller than the library, and went to the office of the clerk, gave him Jennifer Price's name and the year she had died. He managed to find the death certificate in his files, which felt like some kind of Christmas miracle to me.

The line for "Next of Kin" was blank.

It was as if there was as little record of Jennifer Price's death as there was of her life. I'd spoken to Tom Gorman on my way to New Ashford and he said he'd actually tracked down a few of her classmates at Whitesboro College and said that not one of them had stayed in touch with Jennifer Price after she'd left school.

I sat in the car and called the Cheshire Police Department and told the officer who answered the phone that it was a nonemergency, that I was a licensed private investigator from Boston working on a case, even that I was the daughter of a BPD detective.

"That last piece of information just made you a new friend," Officer Davenport said.

I told him about Jennifer Price and how her name had come up in a case I was working and how she had died. He said that because of the year, the record of her death would have been filed, not digitalized.

"And the world was better because of it," I said.

"You can say that again, ma'am," he said.

I told him that I'd wait for his call and if he ever ma'am-ed me again, we were going to have a problem.

He laughed.

"What are you really looking for?" Davenport said.

"Who found the body and called it in," I said.

"You in a rush?" he said.

"I've got nothing going except a big night out in New Ashford," I said.

"No such thing," Davenport said.

It took him only fifteen minutes to find the report. He said the woman who found her was Melinda Salzman, and gave me her address.

"It's not a big town," I said.

"Picked up on that myself," he said.

"Would you know if Melinda Salzman is alive or dead?" I said.

"She passed a while ago," he said. "Couldn't tell you what year, exactly."

I was about to thank him for his time when he said, "But you're in luck. Her daughter still lives here."

"You know her daughter?"

"My cousin used to date her," Davenport said. "Her dad, Melinda's husband, was the only doctor in New Ashford. Her daughter ended up marrying the guy who's now the best doctor around here."

Small town, I thought, *getting smaller all the time.*

"Elissa, that's her name, and she and her husband even live in the house she grew up in," Davenport said. "You want her number?"

"The way my day has gone?" I said. "You have no idea how much."

He gave it to me. I put him on speaker and punched it into my phone.

I said, "Turns out my father was right all along."

"How so?" Davenport said.

"The policeman *is* my friend."

He barked out another laugh.

"Serve and protect," he said. "Even in the boonies."

It was Elissa Salzman Stein who told me about the child.

SIXTY-ONE

She was waiting for me outside a lovely brick ranch that seemed to stretch out in all directions. Maybe there are homes as nice in New Ashford. I couldn't imagine there were any nicer than this.

Elissa was small, with long, dark hair that reminded me of Susan Silverman's, a nice figure, wearing white jeans that fit her quite well, a blue linen shirt rolled up to the elbows, cool-looking cork sandals.

"Wow, Jennifer Price," she said after we'd shaken hands. "That's a name that hasn't come up lately."

"I get a lot of that," I said.

She walked me into a long, sunny living room, one that ended with a window looking onto a pretty spectacular view of what I now knew was Sheeps Heaven Mountain. I told her as quickly as I could why I was looking for information about Jennifer Price. Every time I told it, it sounded more complicated, as if I was trying to catch somebody up on *Succession* after they'd missed the first two seasons.

"But you think her death might somehow be connected to Melanie Joan Hall?" she said.

"Call it an operating theory," I said.

Then she asked if I'd like some iced tea she'd just brewed up herself, mixed with homemade lemonade and pretty damn delicious if she did say so herself. She turned out to be right.

Elissa told things her way, almost in reverse. About how the first she'd ever heard of Jennifer Price was probably one night when she was in high school. She was watching TV in this very room with her mom, her dad dead of a heart attack by then, and one of those PSAs for suicide awareness came on. Her mom told Elissa about the young librarian who'd kept to herself, but whom Melinda Salzman, a member of the library board, had finally convinced to join her reading group.

It was, according to Elissa's mother, the one place where she seemed to come alive.

"They met at the library one afternoon a week," Elissa said. "But she didn't show up one afternoon, and Mrs. Baum, the head librarian, said she hadn't come to work that

336

day, which never happened."

Melinda Salzman, her daughter said, tried to call Jennifer Price's house. No answer. Mrs. Baum said Jennifer had never missed a day of work. Melinda drove over to the house. Jennifer's car was out front. The front door was open.

Melinda Salzman found her in the bathtub.

What she also found that day was a stroller and a crib.

"Mom said that until that moment, she had no idea that Jennifer Price was a mom," Elissa said. "Neither did Mrs. Baum. But she kept to herself, and lived in what my mom said wasn't much more than a cabin, on the edge of land up the mountain belonging to the Forestry Service. My mom said it was her way of having one foot in civilization and one in isolation."

"Does anybody live there now?" I said.

"It was abandoned a long time ago," she said, "when the Forestry Service reclaimed the land it was on. I think it's remained empty, but I've heard some talk that they might use it for a new substation if the state ever finds money under the bed, because the house is largely intact."

"Back to the baby," I said. "Boy or girl?"

"Mom said there were no baby clothes,"

Elissa said. "The only thing that she assumed was when Jennifer decided to end
her life, she must have put the baby someplace safe, or up for adoption."

"Where?" I said.

"Mom said it could have been a convent
or orphanage or some foster program,"
Elissa said. "But when the police checked
her phone records after she died, there was
nothing to indicate which one."

"There was a baby," I said. "I had no
idea."

"Sounds like no one did," Elissa said.
"Mom said that haunted her even more
than everybody missing signs with her that
maybe they wouldn't have missed if they'd
gotten to know her better."

"Did they check back with Whitesboro
College?" I said. "It's where she'd gone to
school."

"Mrs. Baum told Mom that Jennifer
hadn't listed a college when she applied for
the job," Elissa said. "Just that she'd bowled
her over with how much she loved and knew
about books."

"Mrs. Baum said something similar in the
obit I read about Jennifer," I said.

"It's all so sad," Elissa said. "How alone
she must have been. My mom and Mrs.
Baum packed up Jennifer's belongings, her

books and things, out of respect, Mom said, and stored them in a space the library's always kept at U-Pack, over behind the Purple Pub. Just in case anybody ever came asking about her. Some long-lost relative maybe. It was mostly boxes filled with her books, and some writing journals, and her clothes."

"Did the police think there might have been a suicide note in there?" I said.

"They said that people don't hide notes like that," Elissa said.

"What about the journals?" I said.

"My mom started to read one of them," she said. "From college. It read like a short story, she said, but rang awfully true. Mom said it was so sad, she had to stop, without any urge to read further. She felt as if she were invading Jennifer's privacy, even though that always sounded counterintuitive to me, because my mother was so regretful she hadn't known more about her."

"Did anybody ever show up to claim her stuff?" I said.

"Somebody did, as a matter of fact," Elissa said. "Mrs. Baum told me. She was still at the library. A woman who said she was a friend of Jennifer's came around asking about her. Mrs. Baum told her where Jennifer's belongings were. She said the last she knew was that the woman was on her way over to collect them."

"I'm guessing Mrs. Baum never mentioned the woman's name?"

She shook her head.

"I'm sorry," Elissa said. "Whoever that person was, she was already long gone by the time Mrs. Baum told my mom she'd even been in New Ashford."

She sighed.

"How much pain must she have been in to give up a child?" Elissa said. "What do you suppose happened to it? I beg your pardon. To him, or her?"

I told her I was going to find out.

"You sound pretty certain," she said.

"Call it another operating theory," I said.

"Is there anybody still around who might possibly be able to help you?" she said.

I told her that just off the top of my head, I could think of one person.

SIXTY-TWO

"Surprised to see me?" I asked when she opened the door.

"As a matter of fact, yes," Holly Hall said.

The name had begun to sound sillier and sillier to me.

"What are you doing here?" she said.

"You neglected to tell me that your late and extremely horny husband got Jennifer Price pregnant before she left town," I said.

"I'm sure I have no idea what you're talking about," she said.

She started to shut the door. I was wearing Dr. Martens boots with extremely sturdy toes. I put my foot out to stop her.

"This is not a moment when you want to annoy me," I said. "You saw how that went with your old friend Lisa."

"You think you can force yourself into my home?" she said.

"You bet!" I said.

"I could call someone."

341

"Please do," I said. "While you're doing that I'll call Tom Gorman and give him an idea for an interesting piece he might write about a certain dead professor, and the former student who killed herself over him. And either gave away their child or worse. You hearing this, Holly? It's starting to sound like a bad Melanie Joan novel, as redundant as that probably sounds to you."

She turned and walked ahead of me into the house. I asked how her trip had gone. She said it was none of my goddamn business. I asked where she'd gone. She gave the same answer.

"And here I thought we'd been bonding," I said.

"Obviously you're not the detective you think you are," she said.

She sat down on the sofa, motioned me into one of the chairs across from it.

"Let's get this over with," she said. "I've got somewhere I need to be."

She was wearing a T-shirt and bike shorts that showed off legs that looked even longer than they did in jeans.

"He got her pregnant," I said. "The timeline makes perfect sense. He got her pregnant and rejected her, and the baby, and she left."

She stared at me, expressionless.

"He knew why she left and I'm sure he told you, even though you neglected to mention that to me," I said.

"I honestly don't know where she ended up," Holly said.

"But I do," I said. "A little dot of a town on the map called New Ashford, Mass. About three hours from here. I know because I just drove here from there."

I smiled.

"How am I doing so far?" I said.

"Swell," she said. "But I didn't keep track of all of my late husband's ex-girlfriends."

"Would it be all right with you if I keep going?" I said.

"Do I have a choice?"

"Nah."

"I saw a picture of her," I said. "Jennifer Price. An old staff picture on one of the library walls. The one where she was working when she slit her wrists. That day when I showed up here, and the old fool collapsed, he thought I was her, didn't he?"

She shook her head, almost sadly.

"Didn't he?" I said.

My tone got her attention.

"Maybe he did," she said. "And maybe he didn't."

"As much screwing around as he did with college girls," I said, "getting one pregnant

343

would have been a game-changer, wouldn't it, even in the more permissive times you so wistfully remember?"

"I suppose," she said.

"Gotta admit, Holly, you sold yourself short as a storyteller," I said. "Because you made up a bunch of bullshit about Jennifer Price, didn't you? The one he loved and lost?"

"I may have mentioned this before," she said. "But he thought he loved us all." She looked at her watch. "There was no reason to tell you the truth, frankly. At that point I was only interested in getting rid of you. I would have said anything."

I leaned forward, elbows on knees, hands clasped together. Firmly. I stared at her, as if she were the one coming into complete focus now.

"He didn't care about his own child, did he?" I said.

She started to say something, then hesitated. I studied her even more closely, looking for some kind of tell. But got none.

"He told me that she called him once, after the child was born," Holly said.

"Was it a boy or girl?" I said.

"I'm not sure he even asked," she said. "He told me that he told *her* to never call him again, that she'd never meant anything to him, he thought he'd made that clear before she left Whitesboro."

Holly Hall gave a tiny roll of her shoulders. "And then she died," she said.

"How did the son of a bitch even know that?" I said.

"He said a friend of hers called," she said. "A woman. She said Charles's number was one of just a few Jennifer had in her Filofax."

"Did you ever ask what had happened to the child?"

"Why would I?" she said. "Jennifer had always been his problem, not mine. Why should I have cared about her kid?"

"Why, indeed?" I said.

Then I was up and out of my chair and leaning across the coffee table and slapping her across the face.

Before she could say anything, I said, "That was for you *and* your husband."

"I'm tired of people slapping me," she said. "Now, get the hell out of my house."

I could see her face reddening where I'd hit her, same as it had with Lisa Karlin at the gym that day. But she hadn't touched the place with her hand, or moved.

"One more question."

"How many ways do I have to tell you that I'm done talking to you?"

"Did Jennifer Price write a book?" I said.

345

And Holly Hall smiled.

"That's all you care about, isn't it?" she said. "Not the poor, tortured little flower. Not what happened to a missing child. Just your awful client."

"Humor me," I said.

"She wrote something," Holly Hall said. "I don't know if it was a *book* book. But whatever it was, *it* was the reason she left, not the pregnancy."

"And why is that?"

"Charles said that the only way to get her out of his life was to tell her she had no talent," she said. "That the only reason he ever told her she did have talent was to get her into bed. There. Are you happy now?"

"Not one single part of this makes me happy," I said.

"Charles told her that he couldn't believe he'd ever wasted his time on her in the first place," she said. "*That* was when poor Jennifer left."

SIXTY-THREE

I felt like I had been in the car for twenty-four hours straight since leaving Boston, but decided to use the trip back productively, by making phone calls.

And as tired as I was, I felt as if I'd done some real detecting today. It felt very good, even if it dealt with such a sad and terrible story.

I knew that in the morning I would find out everything I possibly could about adoptive records in the state of Massachusetts, starting my search in the western part of the state and then expanding it from there. It would probably be a waste of time, just because the adoption may not have been in Massachusetts, as close as New Ashford was to New York and New Hampshire and maybe even Vermont. And I wasn't sure how finding out what had happened to Jennifer Price's child might get me to where I wanted to go.

Maybe I just wanted to continue to hope that she hadn't killed that child before killing herself.

I tried Tom Gorman first, but the call went straight to voicemail, the purgatory of the technological world. Called the paper and was told that he had taken a rare vacation week. Cape Cod, his assistant said. I asked to be directed to his voicemail there and left this message:

"A vacation without *me*? And so close to Boston?"

Knowing that would get him going.

I called Melanie Joan then and told her about my trip to New Ashford and then about what I had learned from the widow Hall.

"I told you she was a royal bee-atch," Melanie Joan said.

She sounded far more engaged about that than about the child Jennifer Price had had with her first ex-husband.

"I believe I've mentioned to you before that when it comes to men, you sure can pick 'em," I said.

"You've actually mentioned that on multiple occasions," she said. "But might I mention to *you* that making mean comments about the men in my life doesn't get us any closer to finding out who is after me?"

"Well," I said, "you've got me there."

"Listen," she said, "I'm about to go out to dinner with Spike and Samantha, and my face isn't nearly done."

She made it sound like a pot roast that wasn't ready to come out of the oven.

I was past Springfield, and about to make one more gas stop, having forgotten to fill the tank before leaving Whitesboro.

"Before you run," I said, "I've got one last question about your NDA with Charles Hall."

"My God," she said. "Are we back to that?"

"Somebody has been killing people around you and still might be coming for you," I said. "Try to keep that in mind."

"Do you honestly think it might be Holly?" she said. "Because I'm about to cut her off?"

"Just one more alternative theory," I said. "It's why I want to know exactly when your lawyers might have informed Holly that the money wasn't going to keep rolling in forever."

"I don't remember when exactly," she said. "But it was Richard who called one day and asked if I was aware that the money was to keep being sent unless one of us died. Does it matter?"

"I asked Holly if the money kept coming after Charles was dead when I became aware of the NDA," I said. "She told me that there might be some dispute about that."

"Then her lawyers didn't read it closely enough," Melanie Joan said.

"Or perhaps they did," I said.

Then I said, "Melanie Joan, might Jennifer Price have written a book while she was Charles's student?"

Her answer was loud enough that I immediately had to lower the volume on Car-Play.

"If she did, it wasn't mine!" Melanie Joan said. "Now, good*bye!*"

I stopped for gas and bought myself a giant Dunkin' coffee, and decided to put on Springsteen for the rest of the ride home.

Even as I was driving up Storrow Drive my brain was back in New Ashford, at Elissa Salzman's house, which had once belonged to Melinda, who had found the body of Jennifer Price at a small, isolated house in the woods. The same Jennifer Price who had once been Charles Hall's pregnant mistress, and who might have written the book that eventually became *A Girl and Not a God.* Which Melanie Joan denied, just not to the death if I had anything to say about it. But if her first novel had really been Jennifer Price's, then Melanie Joan had been lying to me from the start, trying to protect an ass that Hawk thought might be starting to head south.

I thought: *Who was the friend who had come for Jennifer Price's belongings, all those years after she'd died?*

Bruce was singing "Thunder Road" by now. The song made me smile, for the first time all day. So did the knowledge, as I made the turn off Storrow, that Rosie the dog was waiting for me.

SIXTY-FOUR

Spike went on Melanie Joan's morning walk with her. He said he'd offered that exciting opportunity to Hawk, who'd told him that walking was part of his exercise routine only when he was making his way from the weights to the heavy bag at Henry Cimoli's gym.

Spike said he'd take that as a no and Hawk said, "More like a fuck no."

Before they'd left, and while Melanie Joan was upstairs trying to decide which pair of Lululemon pants to wear, I asked Spike if Melanie Joan had set the plan yet for her and Samantha to leave for New York.

He laughed.

"Melanie Joan making a plan?" he said. "Good one there, Sunny, no shit."

An hour later I was at my desk, making my way through the hell of trying to find out what might have happened to a child given up all that time ago without even knowing *if* the child had been given up for adoption, without even knowing the sex of the child, or the state in which it might have been given up for adoption. I kept thinking about a case Jesse Stone had worked on a couple years ago when a baby a mother didn't want had been left in a dumpster.

If I wanted to do a really deep dive on this, without it occupying all of my waking hours, I might need to hire a hotshot lawyer. Maybe Rita Fiore, red-haired hellcat, might be willing to help me out if I could get her to stop bopping Jesse long enough.

At a little before noon, I called Hawk and asked him if he wanted to have lunch with me.

"Where?" he said.

"You pick."

"Capital Grille on Boylston," Hawk said.

"Do we need a reservation?" I said.

"You might, missy," he said. "I don't."

I was getting ready to take the long walk from the office across the Common and the Public Garden down Boylston, all the way to where the Capital Grille was, next to the Hynes Convention Center, when my mail was delivered.

The letter from Dr. John Melvin was included.

After reading it I called Hawk and told

him I was going to need a raincheck on
lunch.

SIXTY-FIVE

Frank Belson said, "You buying this?"

"It's his handwriting," I said. "And the very last thing he said to me was that someday all of my questions would be answered."

"What about that missing manuscript you've been chasing around?" Belson said. "The shitheel doesn't address that in his letter."

"Beats the hell out of me, Frank," I said. "Maybe I had three cases going instead of one, and the book had nothing to do with murders and shootings and the whole damn thing."

I was still in my office. Belson had said he'd come to me. Now he had read what I had read in Melvin's letter. It didn't address whom he'd hired to do the killings. Melvin said that was his gift to Frank Belson and me, leaving us one last puzzle to solve. But he wrote that he *had* made it his mission, as he had gotten older in prison and come to the realization, despite his series of appeals, that he was going to die there, to get even with everyone who had put him in that cell.

He decided to hurt Melanie Joan, he wrote, by hurting those close to her. He had sent the shooter after Melanie Joan and me when we were out in the open that day, as a way of ending things. Maybe, he wrote, because of a premonition that his days were numbered.

And he wrote that all of us who'd put him away would wonder if someone might be coming for us after he was gone, because the shooter had twice failed.

"The game continues" is the way the letter ended.

"Asking you again," Belson said. "You believe him?"

"That hitters are going to keep coming?" I said. "I do not. Do I believe the rest of it? I have to say it's a pretty convincing closing argument. Either way, I think he knew he was dying and wanted to get in his last licks before he did."

Belson said, "He could've orchestrated it from inside. Been done before. Without a single goddamn thing showing up in his phone records." He shrugged. "He had a way of knowing what was happening on the outside. Not crazy to think that the crazy bastard found out about somebody sending those chapters and thinking he had an opening to drive everyfuckingbody crazy."

"Going back into the phone records wouldn't give you a road map?" I said.

Belson snorted. "Are you shitting? There should be a new cell phone company for phones these guys manage to get their hands on in the joint."

"I wouldn't put any of this by him," I said.

"A prison rat like him," Belson said, "maybe he'd pissed off too many people in Concord. And needed to start settling scores before it was too late. Especially after those appeals kept getting slam-dunked. Or maybe it was Doyle finding a way to settle his own score with him."

"A serial killer from behind bars," I said.

Belson nodded. "I read about this guy in Arizona one time. Looking at the needle. I forget what the body count was out there. He wasn't even using the same guy to settle his scores."

I nodded at the letter, sitting there in a plastic baggie on my desk.

"What will you do with the letter?" I said.

"Give it to my immediate superior, bless her heart," he said. "Who will give it to her superior, and so on and so forth. I doubt they'll release it. Or maybe they'll want people to know Melvin confessed. Who the fuck knows? But I think it's enough for them to close the books on the lawyer and the editor."

"And we might never know for sure," I said. "You okay with that?"

He picked up the baggie. I grinned watching him stick the unlit cigar into the side pocket of his raincoat.

"Some old baseball manager said one time that you win some, you lose some, and sometimes you get rained out," he said.

"You know how I love baseball expressions," I said.

"I got more," he said.

"Maybe next time," I said.

SIXTY-SIX

Hawk had passed on dinner at the house, saying he had plans with the redhead. I arranged to meet up with him tomorrow and pay him out of the big check Melanie Joan had presented to me before dinner, one that I planned to divide up equally among him and Spike and me.

"Well, thank you for your service, as people like to say," I said to Hawk.

"What people?" he said.

There was a pause at his end and then he said, "You sure we done here, missy? You good with your pen pal?"

"You're not?" I said.

"Not ready to put a bow on this even if you might be," he said. "On account of I's still reporting to a higher power."

"God?" I said.

"Susan," he said.

I laughed and asked him again if he was sure he didn't want to have dinner with

Melanie Joan and Samantha and Spike and me.

"Fuck no," he said.

Spike cooked, lemon chicken and fingerling potatoes and broccolini. Now we were having coffee in the living room, still talking about John Melvin's letter.

"I knew John hated me," Melanie Joan said. "I just didn't know how much he hated me."

"So you do believe his deathbed confession?" I said.

I'd made a copy of it for her.

"It needed an editor," Melanie Joan said. "But yes, I do."

"He waited an awfully long time to get even," I said.

"Sustained by hate," Samantha said. "Or rage."

"Or both," I said.

"Revenge," Spike said. "A dish served cold." He grinned. "I just made that up, by the way."

Melanie Joan laughed and leaned over and kissed him on the cheek. She wanted the evening to be festive, a celebration of what she had decided was closure.

"Do you really no longer care who sent those pages?" I said to her. "It's kind of where we all came in, Melanie Joan."

"You want to know what I really think?" she said.

"Always," I said.

"I think whoever did it just changed their mind when people around me started dying," she said.

"Maybe it makes as much sense as anything else," Samantha Heller said. "You've probably made enemies you didn't even know were enemies, long before even I came along."

"Fame is a cruel mistress," Spike said. He grinned. "Just came up with that, too."

"I'm begging you to stop," I said.

He went into the kitchen then and came back with glasses and a bottle of Louis XIII cognac he'd brought from the restaurant, and poured for everybody.

"To Melanie Joan," Spike said. "A survivor."

We all drank to that.

"Tell the truth," he said to Melanie Joan. "Are you going to miss me when you're finally back in Tinseltown?"

She and Samantha had decided to skip publisher meetings in New York for now. They were flying back to Los Angeles from the private terminal at Hanscom Field tomorrow. Samantha said that even with John Melvin dead, they were hiring L.A.

bodyguards for the immediate future to be on the safe side, and maybe even for Boston when the new series started shooting in a few months.

"I am going to miss you desperately," Melanie Joan said to Spike. "And Hawk, too."

She turned to me.

"Do you really think this is over?" she said, and sipped cognac.

"For you, perhaps," I said. "I very much want it to be for you. But I still want to know what happened to Jennifer Price's baby."

"If you ever do find out," Melanie Joan said, "let me know."

"I thought you didn't care about her," I said.

"Oh, I don't care about poor tragic Jennifer or her baby, as insensitive as that might sound," she said. "But the more I think about that baby, the more I think it might be the start of a good novel." She winked at me. "Or the end of one. After all, I need a good idea for my next book whenever Samantha and I do meet with publishers."

She drank more cognac. She'd had plenty of wine at dinner and was starting to act more than somewhat lit. And as full of herself as ever.

"Maybe I should keep you on retainer to keep searching," Melanie Joan said.

"You don't have to," I said. "If I want to find what happened to that child, I will, I promise you."

It came out with more force than I intended. I saw Samantha Heller staring at me.

"You know something?" she said. "I believe you."

She and Melanie Joan left late the next morning in Samantha's rental car, Samantha saying that the nice thing about private terminals was how they magically made rental cars disappear. I made two trips out to the car with Melanie Joan's bags. What we couldn't fit in the trunk we put in the backseat.

Melanie Joan and I hugged it out at the front door, and she said that she could never properly thank me. I told her I still wasn't quite sure what exactly I'd done for her.

"I'm here, aren't I?" she said, and then kissed me on both cheeks.

I hugged Samantha Heller, too.

"I wish I could say this has been fun," I said.

She laughed.

"I hear *that,* girl," she said. "But if I ever get into trouble of my own . . ."

I finished the thought for her.

"Call Spike," I said. "Or Hawk."

I was upstairs painting that afternoon, on my way to pay Hawk, when Samantha called.

"You guys couldn't even go a whole day without talking to me?" I said.

"It turns out we took a little side trip," Samantha said. "But I'll let the writer explain. She's quite proud of herself."

They were on speaker.

"I found Jennifer Price's daughter," Melanie Joan said now. "I'll explain when you get here."

"Wait," I said. "Where are you guys?"

"Sheeps Heaven Mountain," Melanie Joan said.

SIXTY-SEVEN

It was what had been Jennifer Price's house, her cabin, halfway up the mountain, the one that had recently been reclaimed by the Forestry Service, according to Elissa Salzman. It was just starting to get dark by the time I got there. By now I was starting to think my car could have self-driven itself to New Ashford and back.

Somehow, against all odds, the address Samantha had given me worked on Waze, even though when I got off Route 7 I felt as if I were participating in some sort of off-road race.

Samantha's rental car was out front, in what must have been a small front yard once, now overgrown with wildflowers and bushes and scrub. But there was a light coming from inside. I had no way of telling whether it was a lamp or a high-powered flashlight.

Samantha must have seen the headlights

of my car coming up the narrow road, because she came outside, smiling and shaking her head. She was wearing a down vest and jeans and what looked to be hiking boots.

"Was it you or Spike that said Melanie Joan wasn't much for plans, I forget?" she said.

"Definitely Spike."

"Well, our girl certainly had one on the way to the private plane," Samantha said. "Somehow she took you saying you were going to find out about that baby as a challenge. Like it was some kind of contest. And Melanie Joan, being Melanie Joan, just had to be the smartest girl in class."

"Trust me," I said. "It's a lifelong affliction."

"It only took her one day to solve the mystery," Samantha said. "But I'll let her tell you, or she'll probably fire me."

I was walking ahead of her into the cabin when I felt the needle go into the back of my neck, and she was grabbing me by the hair.

As I started to sag, I could see the razor blade Samantha had in front of my throat.

From behind me she whispered, "I'm Jennifer Price's daughter."

SIXTY-EIGHT

Dr. John Melvin had drugged me once, but I had been ready for it that time, had taken an antidote before he did, and knew that Richie Burke, gun in hand, was waiting outside the door to help me take him down. Which we did.

This was different. I had been out cold. Now I was awake again, facing Melanie Joan, both of us duct-taped to chairs, duct tape over her mouth and not mine. Samantha Heller, or whatever her real name was, had been pacing and talking in a manic way for a while, about being abandoned and about the foster-home hell of a childhood, always circling back to how it all began when Melanie Joan stole her mother's book and ruined her life.

Every time she would say that, Melanie Joan would violently shake her head.

Samantha still had the long razor in her hand, waving it in the air occasionally to emphasize one of her points.

"I was going to wait a little while longer, Sunny," she said. "But when you said last night you were going to find the baby, I knew you were telling the truth. And you would find your way to me eventually."

She laughed and seemed to become even more manic.

"The thing is," she said, "I needed you to understand. Because I like you, Sunny. I think you are a good, well-intentioned person, even if I can't let you leave here. But I needed you to understand. You understand *that,* don't you?"

She stopped in front of me and spoke next in a soft voice.

"You can scream if you want to," she said. "No one will hear. I just taped up her mouth because I am so sick and *fucking* tired of listening to her."

"I don't scream," I said.

I looked at Melanie Joan. I noticed the way Samantha had tied her wrists to the arms of the chair.

Facing up.

There was a stack of yellow pages on the table in what had been the kitchen once.

My own wrists were taped so tightly to the sides of my own chair my hands were starting to lose circulation.

Samantha walked over to Melanie Joan now and said, "I am going to take the tape off your mouth. But if you continue to annoy me, I will cut you now and let you bleed out the way my mother did.

"Are we clear?" Samantha continued.

Melanie Joan's eyes were as crazy as Samantha Heller's, just with fear. But she nodded. Then Samantha reached over and ripped the tape off her mouth, the sound harsh, echoing in the small front room where perhaps Jennifer Price had once rocked Samantha to sleep.

Samantha turned back to me.

"You want to know the amazing thing, Sunny?" she said. "She'd still rather die than admit she stole my mother's book."

"I told you I didn't steal it!" Melanie Joan yelled. *"Charles gave it to me!"*

And there it was.

"He told me he had written it!" Melanie Joan said. She sighed. "It's why I paid him all those years."

Samantha slapped her hard across the face, Melanie Joan's head whipping to the side. Then again.

"Liar," she said in the soft voice again.

"It's the truth," Melanie Joan said. She started to cry now. "He told me that it wasn't very good, but I had the talent to

369

make it into something."

"And why would he *do* something like that?" Samantha said.

"To sleep with me!" Melanie Joan said, crying harder now.

"Well, isn't that ironic, if it is true?" Samantha said. "Since the one whose life got fucked because of it was me."

Then she was pacing again, and rambling, about how long it took her to find out who her birth mother was, and how she finally tracked her here, and how she convinced them that she and Jennifer Price had been friends back in upstate New York. And how it was after she took possession of the belongings that she found the manuscript.

"She died before she even saw Melanie Joan's book, didn't she?" I said.

"But I found *her* book," she said. "In with some others she started and abandoned. It looks like she became almost obsessive about her writing the last couple years of her life."

I said, "And some of those pages were similar to Melanie Joan's book."

"It wasn't Melanie Joan's book! It was my mother's!"

Keep her talking.

"But how did you find out everything that had happened to Jennifer Price?"

370

"That's the best part!" she said, too brightly. "My fucking father *told* me!"

She said, "Even after what he did to her, she dedicated the book to him. And when I went back to that shitty little college to find him, the old fool was so far around the bend that he thought I was her and spilled his pathetic guts."

"He didn't think I was your mother when I showed up at his house," I said. "He thought I was you."

"Who knows what people are thinking when they're not thinking," she said.

"You got yourself a job at the publishing house," I said. Almost talking to myself now.

"Chaz Blackburn was as much of an old lech as my father," she said. "It was like shooting fish in a barrel, to use a tacky cliché, getting him to hire me. I was like one of my father's girls."

I said, "And then you became an agent, you were already in that world."

"Good girl, Sunny!" Samantha said. "And then I, lo and behold, I was the agent to the great Melanie Joan Hall, who wanted someone she could trust."

She smiled. But there was nothing normal about it. It was more like a Halloween mask smile.

"People like me, Sunny," she said. "You did."

"So this was all about revenge," I said. "For you and for John Melvin."

"Spike was right about the best way to serve it," she said.

She looked at me.

"Stop twisting your wrists, Sunny. Or I *will* cut you."

"Why haven't you just killed us already and left?" I said.

"Because you both need to understand, for fuck's sake!"

"John Melvin lied about being behind it all," I said.

"Like a champion," Samantha Heller said. "Made it so much easier for me to get her in the trunk after I went to the needle with her."

She paced and talked a little more, some of it impossible to follow and some of it making her pathology completely logical, at least to her, about how Melanie Joan needed to suffer the way she had. And how she was going someplace where nobody would ever be able to find her. She had wanted this. Her big scene. And I had walked right into it.

I thought: *She makes John Melvin look sane.*

I remember being in a room like this once before, listening to Bobby Toms, Felix Burke's son, tell us all about it, as if he was the one who had waited his whole life to do that. Susan Silverman told me at the time about that particular pathology, the need for people to explain themselves and be the heroes of their own dramas, which always made perfect sense to them. I thought I was going to die that night, too, and didn't. Maybe you got lucky that way only once.

I heard something outside then.

But so did she.

Samantha walked past Melanie Joan and casually cut one of her wrists.

Melanie Joan began to shriek, staring down at the blood.

Then Samantha was quickly behind me and had the razor to my throat.

"Whoever is out there needs to come inside now," she called out. "And if I see a weapon, I will sadly be forced to slit Sunny's throat."

Thirty seconds later Hawk came walking through the door, tossing his Magnum in ahead of him.

SIXTY-NINE

Hawk winked at me and then whistled softly.

"My, my, if we don't got ourselves a situation here," he said.

"Melanie Joan has ten minutes before she bleeds out," Samantha said. "Fifteen, tops. So it would be best if you don't do something stupid, Hawk."

"Always made it my habit not to do stupid," Hawk said. "And I's more concerned about missy here than Melanie Joan."

Samantha said to me, "There was no reason for you to have him follow you." She looked almost angry. "There was nothing suspicious about that phone call to Sunny."

"She didn't," Hawk said. "When I got that message from her she was comin' out here, it didn't make no sense to me. And then, being the curious mother*fucker* that I am, I call out there to Hanscom, and found out there was never no plane to Hollywood."

She pressed the tip of the razor harder against my throat. I thought I might be bleeding. She had killed two people this way. She knew how to do it. And there was nothing Hawk could do from across the room to stop it.

I saw Melanie Joan's head fall forward. There was so much blood on her white jeans.

"You can't just let her die," I said to Samantha.

"Watch me," she said.

"Whatever you do," Hawk said, "you got to know you ain't walkin' out the room alive. I'll take what you got there in your hand and fillet you like a fuckin' fish."

"This has nothing to do with you, Hawk," Samantha said.

I was wondering how many minutes it had been since she'd cut Melanie Joan Hall's wrist. And how good Samantha Heller's math was on her bleeding out.

"See there, now," Hawk said, his voice still soft. "You don't know nothin' about me."

Then, for a moment, the room was like a still-life, the only dominant sound the harsh, shallow breathing from Melanie Joan Hall.

"Nobody else has to die, Samantha," I said. "We can get you help."

"Like the help my mother got?" she said.

"Let Hawk attend to Melanie Joan," I said, "and then we can talk about this."

"She done talkin', missy," Hawk said, eyes still focused on the razor.

"Hawk's right," Samantha said.

Then, in this sad, almost tired voice, she said, "I'm so sorry, Sunny."

In the next moment the knife was off my throat and she was slashing it across her own, knowing how to do it one last time, and then it was ending for her the way it had ended here for her mother.

SEVENTY

I sat with Melanie Joan in what could only be described as our living room at this point. Her right wrist was still bandaged. She was already talking about having her plastic surgeon do something about the scar when the bandage came off. She had survived Samantha Heller's attack, but barely, the EMTs getting to her in time from the Berkshire Medical Center about ten miles away.

Samantha Heller was dead before the ambulance got there, effectively gone by the time she hit the floor.

Now Melanie Joan's suitcases were once again lined up near the front door like good soldiers, while she waited for the limousine that would take her to Hanscom Field, where she would board the private jet that had really been ordered this time.

She had been telling me about the things Samantha had told her before I had arrived,

377

about her being raped by one of her stepfathers, and the life she had fabricated for herself once she was old enough, the one about growing up as a child of privilege in Manhattan when in fact she had spent two of her teenage years there in a group home.

She told me again about the razor being held to her throat as she read the things Samantha had wanted her to say to me on the phone, after Samantha had drugged her.

"There are reasons," I said, "and there are excuses. Those are reasons why she snapped when she found out about Jennifer Price."

She sipped some coffee. The car would be here soon. She stared at the bandage as she did.

"I'm sorry I lied to you about the book," she said.

"We've gone over this," I said.

"But you need to know how sorry I am that I *did* lie to the person I'd come running to for protection," she said.

"It wasn't just me you lied to," I said. "You lied to yourself, for a long time."

"But I did believe he was the one who wrote it," she said. "That's the real reason I sent him money for all those years."

She had spent a fair amount of time in tears over the past few days, since I'd driven her back from the Berkshire Medical Center. I was afraid now that she was about to start crying all over again.

"She hated me even more than John Melvin did," Melanie Joan said. "If such a thing is even possible." She sighed and shook her head. "Over a crime she only thought I had committed."

She was on the couch. I was in a chair on the other side of the coffee table, one of hers, with Rosie the dog in my lap.

"I'm very fond of you, Melanie Joan," I said. "I am. I keep telling you that. Rosie and I are living here because of your generosity. But while you may have been, ah, acquitted here, it doesn't mean you're innocent of all charges."

"I'm not sure I understand."

"In the end," I said, "it *wasn't* your work, and it wasn't your story, no matter how much you may have improved it. It was hers. Samantha was right about that, however the material ended up in your hands in the first place."

"I'm not a thief," she said.

I smiled. Couldn't help it.

"Of course not," I said. "You're Melanie Joan Hall."

There was a ping on her phone. The driver was probably close.

"Who had John Melvin killed?" she said.

"Joe Doyle," I said, without even a hint of hesitation.

"My God," she said. "Can you prove that?"

"Not in a million years," I said.

I smiled.

"But my father thinks he can," I said.

"Do you believe John sent that shooter to kill me when we were at the river that day?"

"Yes," I said.

"The only thing that saved us was luck," she said.

"It's the residue of design," I said.

"Who said that?"

I smiled again, at a private joke, at my own expense.

"An old baseball guy," I said.

"I thought you didn't like baseball," she said.

"I don't," I said.

The stretch limousine arrived a few minutes later. I hugged her goodbye, again. She said she'd see me when she was back in Boston, once principal photography began on the new series about the granddaughter of a character born in the imagination of the late Jennifer Price.

"Look forward to it," I lied.

The driver loaded the bags. The car pulled away up River Street Place. I watched it until it disappeared around the corner of Charles, just to make sure she was really leaving. And called Jet Linx ninety minutes later to make sure, as the fancy people say, that the private plane was wheels-up.

I left Susan Silverman a phone message after that, telling her I needed to reschedule tomorrow's appointment because I was headed out of town, but thanking her, profusely, for introducing me to Hawk.

I called Hawk then, but before I could thank him again, he said, "In the middle of something here, missy," and heard a woman giggle as he ended the call.

Finally I called Spike and asked him if he could take care of Rosie while I was away. He asked where I was going. I told him.

"Didn't see that coming," he said.

"Nor did I," I said.

I took the mid-afternoon Jet Blue flight to New York, got into an Uber at LaGuardia. I was staying at The Carlyle, which I could afford, and mightily, thanks to the largesse of the famous author Melanie Joan Hall.

He was waiting for me at the 76th Street entrance.

"Were you surprised to hear from me?" I said.

"Very," he said.

"Are you really as fun a date as you keep

saying you are?" I said. "Because I could use one."

"Just watch me," Tom Gorman said.

"You're sure that's not fake news?" I said to the editor of the *Utica Observer-Dispatch*. He'd already told me on the phone that the reason he'd been at the Cape was to meet with the publisher of *The Boston Globe,* who'd offered him a columnist's job.

For now he smiled at me. The smile was still working for him. Back at the start of this, at The Street Bar that night, I had told my father I was ready for something new.

Or somebody.

"Why don't we go inside and have a martini at Bemelmans Bar and talk about it?" he said.

"We'd be fools not to," I said.

ACKNOWLEDGMENTS

Once again, my thanks to David and Daniel Parker for the high honor of continuing the character of Sunny Randall.

Thanks to the boss, Ivan Held, who officially invited me into the world of my old friend Robert B. Parker.

My immense gratitude to my editor, Danielle Dieterich, who makes me feel as if we've been working together my whole career.

And finally: There could be no finer caretaker for Mr. Parker's work than the great Esther Newberg, and no better friend to me.

ABOUT THE AUTHOR

Robert B. Parker was the author of seventy books, including the legendary Spenser detective series, the novels featuring police chief Jesse Stone, and the acclaimed Virgil Cole/Everett Hitch Westerns, as well as the Sunny Randall novels. Winner of the Mystery Writers of America Grand Master Award and long considered the undisputed dean of American crime fiction, he died in January 2010. **Mike Lupica** is a prominent sports journalist and the *New York Times* bestselling author of more than forty works of fiction and nonfiction. A longtime friend to Robert B. Parker, he was selected by the Parker estate to continue the Sunny Randall series.